"MICHAEL," SHE SAID IN A DREAMY, CONTENTED voice. "Where did you get these extra blankets?"

"They were on the sofa."

Maddy opened her eyes. "But those were for you. You'll never be able to keep warm with just a sheet."

"I'll be okay, Maddy," he said, teeth chattering. "Just get some sleep."

"Listen to you, you're freezing to death. I'll never be able to sleep knowing I took your blankets." She sighed. "Get in the bed, Michael. Hurry, before you catch pneumonia."

He stared at her, slack-jawed, wondering if he'd heard right. "What did you say?"

She pulled the covers aside. "Get in. We'll have to sleep close so we can share our body heat." When he simply stood there, she gave an impatient huff. "Don't just stand there looking at me as though I've grown horns. We're talking survival here."

Michael nodded dumbly and climbed into bed, burrowing beneath the blankets. She turned her back to him and scooted close so they were lying spoon fashion. As he lay there, pressed against her softness, enveloped in her scent, only one coherent thought entered his mind.

*Eureka!*

## WHAT ARE *LOVESWEPT* ROMANCES?

*They are stories of true romance and touching emotion. We believe those two very important ingredients are constants in our highly sensual and very believable stories in the LOVE-SWEPT line. Our goal is to give you, the reader, stories of consistently high quality that may sometimes make you laugh, sometimes make you cry, but are always fresh and creative and contain many delightful surprises within their pages.*

*Most romance fans read an enormous number of books. Those they truly love, they keep. Others may be traded with friends and soon forgotten. We hope that each LOVESWEPT romance will be a treasure—a "keeper." We will always try to publish*

## LOVE STORIES YOU'LL NEVER FORGET
## BY AUTHORS YOU'LL ALWAYS REMEMBER

*The Editors*

# JUST MARRIED
## . . . AGAIN

### CHARLOTTE
### HUGHES

BANTAM BOOKS
*NEW YORK · TORONTO · LONDON · SYDNEY · AUCKLAND*

JUST MARRIED . . . AGAIN

*A Bantam Book / September 1998*

ISBN 0-553-44702-5

*Published simultaneously in the United States and Canada*

PRINTED IN THE UNITED STATES OF AMERICA

OPM      0 9 8 7 6 5 4 3 2 1

Many thanks to attorney Tom Barton
and his lovely wife, Beth, for assisting
with my research

# ONE

Michael Kelly could see Dr. Quigley was peeved about something, and he suspected it had to do with his blood-pressure reading. Although the nurse had already taken it twice, Dr. Quigley had insisted on checking it personally. Finally, the doctor pulled the cuff from his patient's upper arm and glared at him through owlish eyes that had a tendency to bulge when he became upset.

"What's the problem?" Michael said, having grown weary of the doc's accusing looks. He raked his fingers through hair the color of Brazil nuts and fixed the older man with a hard look. It was a tactic he used quite successfully in court to denote his growing impatience with a witness or opposing attorney. Clearly, it said he thought it was time to get the show on the road.

Michael suspected it was all lost on Quigley. The old bear wasn't easily intimidated. He wondered why he continued to use the cantankerous physician when there were plenty of good doctors in the area. Habit, no doubt. Dr. Quigley had been treating the Kelly family for years.

There were times Quigley acted as if Michael were still a kid. It didn't matter that at thirty-three, Michael Kelly had reached a level of success most men struggled toward all their lives. He had already made full partner at Smyth-McGraw, one of the oldest and most respected law firms in Charlotte, North Carolina. With more than one hundred attorneys in residence, Michael was in the higher echelon of lawyers and enjoyed a handsome salary that afforded him Armani suits, Rolex watches, and customized BMWs.

He knew Quigley wouldn't be impressed. The doctor bought his suits at an outlet store, and he bragged that his Volvo station wagon still ran as well as it had when he'd bought it twenty years before. He wouldn't know the difference between a Rolex and a Timex, and he wouldn't care.

Michael knew those things were important at Smyth-McGraw. A client had only to step inside the expansive main lobby with its marble floors and columns and gaze at the oil portraits of the distinguished founding partners to know that he was getting the very best in legal representation. And while Michael conducted himself with the same subdued professionalism exhibited by his colleagues, he could fight dirty when he had to. One newspaper reporter had referred to him as "a street fighter in gentleman's clothes," when Michael had sparred with an older attorney who'd treated him like a first-year law student. Michael had won the case and had proved he could stand his own ground, while at the same time remaining the consummate professional and treating his older opponent with the utmost respect. The opposing attorney had invited Michael to dine with him at his private club afterward and had offered him a position in his firm. Michael, though flattered, had gracefully declined.

He saw that Dr. Quigley was looking through his pharmaceutical reference. "Would you tell me what's wrong?" he said, noting the doctor's spiky, gunmetal-gray eyebrows were drawn together so tightly, they formed a single horizontal slash across his forehead. The last time the doc had given him that look, he'd followed it up with a discussion on safe sex. Michael had been fifteen at the time and too embarassed to admit he was still a virgin.

"Are you trying to kill yourself?" Quigley said. "If that's the case, then I'll have to refer you to a psychiatrist."

"I don't need a psychiatrist," Michael said tersely. "Just tell me what the problem is." He was in the middle of a wrongful-death suit and was expected back at the courthouse in thirty minutes. He didn't have time to play guessing games with the doctor.

"You had your last physical eighteen months ago, and your blood pressure was one ten over eighty. Today, it's sitting at one sixty over one ten." He crossed his arms over his chest. "At this rate you should have a stroke by Thanksgiving."

Michael knew the man tended to overreact. He also coddled his patients. When Michael had had a hernia repair at the age of eleven, he'd been forbidden to play sports for the rest of the summer. Quigley had sent him a collection of Zane Grey novels to pass the time.

"You're telling me I have less than a week of good, quality life left, is that it?"

"This is no joking matter, boy," the doctor said. "In fact, you're lucky you started having those headaches."

"Lucky?" That was a strange thing to say considering the pain he'd been in the past couple of weeks. When the headaches continued to get worse, he figured he had a brain tumor. His first thought was of his soon-to-be ex-wife. Maddy was going to feel guilty as hell for leaving him when she found out how sick he was. Oddly enough, the thought cheered him.

He could just imagine himself lingering, wasting away, and Maddy, with her good heart, nursing him, confessing her unending devotion. Then he remembered her parting shot, something along the line of "eat dirt and die," and decided he might be hoping for too much.

"Most people don't have any warning," Quigley was saying. "They just go about their business while their condition worsens. Next thing they know they're in the hospital." He studied the younger man in silence. "I don't know what's gotten into you, Michael. When did you start smoking? And don't try and deny it, because I smelled it on you the minute I walked through that door."

"I only smoke occasionally," Michael replied. Like when he had a stiff drink to unwind after a grueling day in court, or on those occasional Sundays when he found himself home with too much time on his hands and too many memories whirling about in his head. And then there were those nights his body ached so badly for his wife, he couldn't sleep.

The nights were the hardest. He damn near smoked an entire pack of cigarettes while waiting for the sun to come up.

"And you've gained weight," Quigley added.

"I haven't gained all that much."

"You can make all the excuses you like," the doctor said, "but we both know you let yourself go the minute Maddy walked out."

Michael's jaw suddenly became hard as concrete. His eyes flashed with outrage. "I don't need a lecture, Doc. I just finished one of the biggest trials of my career, and I'm beat. As for my impending divorce, that topic is not open for discussion."

Quigley realized he'd gone too far and backed off. "You've got to stop putting in so many hours," he said, his tone gentler. "You're going to kill yourself if you don't start learning to have a little fun."

Some of the stiffness left Michael. "I've been trying to cut back on my workload," he said, which was true, "and I've recently started jogging again." He knew the doctor was right. He *had* let himself go. But Maddy's leaving ten months earlier had hit him hard, like a locomotive at full speed. He'd been so far down, he never thought he'd get back up. He had no energy for exercise; it was all he could do to drag himself to work and home again. He'd narrowed his priorities down to work and survival.

"I don't think I'm going to be able to help you." Quigley looked sad.

"What?" Michael was surprised. He couldn't believe this was the same doctor who'd had all the answers when he was growing up. Surely he wasn't so ill that

Quigley couldn't fix him up. "Can't you write me a prescription or something?"

"I'm afraid it's not that simple. This sort of thing requires a whole new lifestyle, a commitment to change."

Michael sighed heavily and resisted checking his wristwatch. "Okay, tell me what you want me to do?"

"When was the last time you had a vacation?"

Michael tried to remember. "Maddy and I used to spend an occasional weekend at our mountain cabin." He wasn't about to tell the old doc that he usually dragged his briefcase along with him. He and Maddy had knocked heads more than once over it. She'd had no idea what it was like to work for a big law firm, the hours of billing he was expected to hand in. Even after making full partner, he still put in ten- and twelve-hour workdays, sometimes seven days a week.

"Maybe that's what you need," Quigley said. "A week in the mountains."

"A whole week?" This time Michael frowned.

"Two days isn't going to do it. I'll start you on medication, but I'm prescribing a week to ten days of R and R to go with it." He reached for his prescription pad. "Also, I have some literature I want you to read. It'll give you information on your condition and how to control it."

His *condition*? Michael didn't like the sound of it, didn't like the thought of having limitations when his health had always been excellent. With a twinge of alarm, he looked at the stack of materials Quigley handed him: "Heart Attack and Stroke: Signals and Action," "Smoke and Stroke—Two Things You Can Live

Without," and "Stroke Prevention: The Brain at Risk." Damn, was he really that bad off?

He pondered the idea of staying at the cabin. Maddy had insisted on putting it on the market soon after their separation, but so far they hadn't had any takers. He could probably afford to take some time off over Thanksgiving. Things really slowed down at the office during the holidays. He wouldn't have to worry about Maddy showing up, since she'd claimed often enough that the place held too many bad memories for her. Michael had taken offense. Sure, he'd spent a lot of time working, but they'd had good times as well.

Quigley tore the top sheet from the pad and handed it to him. "I'm giving you a couple of prescriptions that will help lower your blood pressure, and I want you to lose some weight. You need to exercise more—you can take long walks at the cabin—and you'll have to cut back on the alcohol and sodium. I'm afraid you'll have to go on a special diet to reduce dietary saturated fats and cholesterol."

Michael could feel his eyes glazing over. "Could you possibly confuse me any worse than you already have?"

"It's all spelled out in the literature there. I want to see you back in here the Monday following Thanksgiving." He closed Michael's file, and they both started for the door. "Oh, and don't forget to take your camera with you to the mountains. I'll be looking forward to seeing the pictures of your vacation."

Several hours later Maddy Kelly entered Dr. Quigley's office wearing black leggings, a ribbed black-

and-yellow-striped tee, and yellow high-top Reeboks. Her blonde hair fell to her shoulders in natural waves and curls, a hairstyle that was easy to keep, since she usually showered several times a day. She was surprised to find the doctor himself waiting to give her her injection.

"*This* is an honor," she said, pushing up her sleeve the minute she stepped into the examination room. "Where's your nurse?"

"She had some personal business to attend to," Quigley said, swabbing a small area of her upper arm with rubbing alcohol. He gave her the shot and fixed a round Band-Aid in place. "Aren't you a sight for these tired, old eyes," he said. "You look like a bumblebee in that outfit."

Maddy frowned. "I don't like bumblebees, remember?" She'd been stung by one the previous summer and had suffered an allergic reaction. Which explained why she was taking weekly injections and carried a bee-sting kit in her purse wherever she went. While it wasn't likely she'd run into any bees now that the weather had turned cold, she was trying to complete the series of injections that would build up her tolerance to insect venom.

"Sorry, I forgot." He recapped the syringe, broke off the needle, and placed it in a special container. "So, when are you going to run away with me? I've got plane tickets to Greece in my black bag."

Maddy chuckled, and a beguiling dimple puckered her left cheek. "You big flirt. Wait till I tell Sylvia. She's going to take away all your privileges, and you won't be able to see that new grandbaby of yours."

He pretended to scowl. "Who told you I was a grandfather? I'm much too young and handsome for that sort of thing."

"My, but we're feeling our oats today, aren't we?"

They exchanged another minute or two of good-natured banter before Quigley made a note in her file and closed it. "What are you doing for Thanksgiving?"

Maddy hesitated. She wished people would stop asking her that question. It would be the first Thanksgiving without Michael in six years. Her parents had already migrated to their West Palm Beach winter retreat and had undoubtedly taken an entourage with them, so there went any idea of spending a quiet family holiday together. Lord, she was beginning to feel sorry for herself again.

"I don't know," she said after a moment, keeping her voice light so the kindly old doctor wouldn't see how crummy she was feeling over the whole thing. "Several people have invited me to join them and their families."

"The old pity routine, huh?" he said.

Maddy looked up. "What do you mean?"

"I was a single guy once," he said. "Before Sylvia got her claws in me," he added with a chuckle. "Back in medical school. The married interns always felt sorry for me when the holidays came along, and I got more invitations than a slick-talking politician. 'Course, I knew they were only trying to be nice. I always told them I'd already made plans."

"Weren't you lonely?"

"Heck no. But I've always enjoyed my own company. If I had a cabin in the mountains like you, I'd spend all my free time there."

Maddy pondered it. She certainly didn't want to impose on her friends or have them feel sorry for her. "Maybe that's not such a bad idea," she said as she made for the door. "Thanks for the suggestion, Dr. Quigley."

"Don't forget to take your camera if you go," he said, following behind. "I want to see pictures of the place, and I know what a good photographer you are." He pointed to an enlarged photograph of a waterfall hanging on one wall. It was one she'd taken during a solitary hiking weekend in the mountains; she'd had it matted and framed for his sixtieth birthday.

Maddy suddenly remembered it had been months since she'd picked up her camera, and she realized she missed it. "Maybe I will, at that," she said. She gave him a brief hug and hurried out the door.

Several minutes later Quigley's nurse appeared. "Old fool," she said, giving him a nudge with her elbow. "You know what Sylvia said about you getting involved in your patients' private lives."

Quigley patted her on the shoulder. "What Sylvia doesn't know won't hurt her. And don't forget, Martha, you're six months older than me. If I'm old, you're ancient."

"I may be ancient, but at least I keep up with the weather. There's a major storm in Canada, and they're expecting it to come down as far as Asheville. So, what do you have to say about that, you old poop?"

"I couldn't have planned it better if I'd tried," he told her.

# TWO

"Okay, listen up you guys," Maddy said a couple of days later. "There will be no fighting and no running through the cabin." She gave her charges a stern look. "And if I catch either of you chewing on the furniture, you've had it."

Two pairs of brown eyes gazed back at her in nothing less than open adoration. Two reddish-brown tails thumped steadily against the leather seat. It would have taken only a quick smile or a word of encouragement, and the twin dachshunds would have jumped the console and landed in their mistress's lap. It was all Maddy could do to keep from smiling.

"Now then. In the event we get snowed in and I can't walk you—which is a strong possibility—you will cooperate by using the litter box. Accidents will result in lost TV privileges. Oops, I forgot, there's no television at the cabin." Maddy paused when she noticed a station wagon passing. The couple inside stared back at her.

"Look at those people gawking at me," she said.

"Probably think I'm crazy for talking to my dogs. Wonder what they'd think if they knew I read you bedtime stories?" She chuckled and glanced at her pets.

More tail thumping.

Maddy continued down the interstate in her red Jeep Cherokee, noticing the wind and rain had begun to pick up in the last hour or so. The weatherman was calling for a winter storm, but she'd never known it to sleet or snow before January. She was prepared just in case. The ice chest in back held a turkey, steaks for grilling in the fireplace, and a small ham. She'd also packed canned goods and an array of fruits and vegetables. Yep, she could probably make it till Christmas if she had to.

She wondered if she was prepared for the rush of feelings that would hit her once she stepped inside the cabin. Then she fortified her nerves with the thought that after all the pain she'd already suffered, anything now would be minimal.


Michael could see the disappointment in his mother's eyes. She and his sister-in-law, Brenda, had been baking pies and bread all afternoon in preparation for Thanksgiving dinner the following day. His father and oldest brother were in the den watching a football game. Michael had said a quick hello to both of them but hadn't bothered to join them. The two men, both detectives on the force, shared a special camaraderie. Michael always felt as though he was intruding.

"But you've spent every Thanksgiving with your

family," his mother said, giving her son a wounded look. "How can you desert us at a time like this?"

"Now, Mama," Brenda said consolingly as she carried her nine-month-old daughter on one hip and wiped the counters down with her free hand. All her daughters-in-law called her mama or mother. Kathleen Kelly insisted on it. "If the doctor feels Michael needs to get away for health reasons, then we should stand by him. After all, we want Michael to be around for future Thanksgivings," she added.

Michael offered Brenda a smile of appreciation. If anyone could win his mother over, it was his oldest brother's wife. Brenda was a born nurturer. She had tried to comfort him in the early days of his and Maddy's split, but he'd been too proud to admit he was hurting. She often told him he was in denial. If putting in sixteen-hour days and tossing back several shots of Scotch before bedtime could be labeled denial, then her diagnosis had been correct. But he wasn't about to admit as much.

"I suppose you're right," Kathleen Kelly said. It was obvious she loved the younger woman and respected her opinion. She was close to all her boys' wives. She often claimed that after raising five sons, three of whom had grown up to be policemen like their father, her daughters-in-law were a welcome relief. Unquestionably, her grandchildren were the light of her life. "It's kind of late to get started, don't you think? I mean, it's after seven o'clock."

"There'll be less traffic."

Finally, his mother shrugged. "Well, at least let me wrap up a couple of these pies." She started to get up.

"Better not," he said, giving her a grim smile. "Dr. Quigley has me on a diet too."

"That's ridiculous! You're not overweight," she said as Becky, her ten-year-old granddaughter, came into the room asking for something to drink. Brenda reached for a container of apple juice from the refrigerator and poured some into a glass.

It always amazed Michael what women could do with one hand. He tugged his niece's ponytail and made a face at the baby. The older girl smacked his hand, the other giggled and hid her face. "Where's Danny?" he asked, glancing around for some sign of his thirteen-year-old nephew.

Brenda handed the glass of juice to her daughter. "Sulking. He wanted to meet a bunch of his friends at the movies, and his dad and I said no."

"Which they had every right to do," Kathleen said, as if her opinion had been the deciding vote. "His grades are terrible." She stopped abruptly. "Oh, my. Didn't I hear the weatherman mention a possible snow-storm in the mountains?"

Michael chuckled, leaned over, and kissed her on the cheek. "You know it never snows this early in the year, Mom. But if it does, I've packed enough food and blankets to see me through the worst storm." He argued with his mother a few more minutes before bidding them all farewell. Even though he knew he'd miss having Thanksgiving with them, he actually relished the thought of enjoying a little peace and quiet. He knew he was crazy to push himself the way he did, but he also knew the reasons why. He only hoped being at the cabin didn't dredge up memories of Maddy. He'd worked too hard trying to exorcise them from his mind.

Maddy was less than an hour from the cabin when the cold rain changed to sleet. She turned her wipers on high and switched the radio off in order to better concentrate on her driving. In the next seat, her pets slept peacefully. She wished she had gotten an earlier start, but she'd been held up at the gym by a woman who wanted to take off thirty pounds overnight, even though it'd taken her several years to put them on. People didn't enjoy hearing that weight loss and good health took time and hard work; they wanted a miracle cure. As a fitness instructor, Maddy was expected to give them one. She could offer them knowledge and motivation and maybe a few tips, but she could not wave a magic wand and instantly give them the kind of body they desired.

People were never really happy about their bodies. Although years of fitness training kept her in tip-top shape, there were still things she would change about her own body if she could. Her thighs and calves for example. While she wanted them to be trim and shapely, she sometimes felt they were too muscular. She had recently cut back on exercising that part of her body.

Michael, on the other hand, claimed she had the longest, shapeliest legs he'd ever seen, and he'd always insisted on her wrapping them around his waist when they made love. Maddy felt something flutter inside her stomach at the thought of her soon-to-be ex-husband.

Lovemaking had always been especially good between them; in fact, they'd spent almost every waking moment in the sack when they'd first married. But after several years Michael had begun to feel too tired for sex. He fell asleep as soon as his head hit the pillow. Maddy had ordered sexy lingerie from various catalogs and pranced about in garter belts and feathered boas, but nothing seemed to work.

She and Michael had become little more than roommates, their conversations superficial and banal.

She knew her marriage was in trouble long before she missed her first period. That was nothing compared with what she went through after telling Michael she was pregnant.

Maddy was suddenly jolted from her thoughts when she realized the sleet had turned to snow. All at once the wet stuff became white and slightly powdery, like confectioners' sugar. She was glad to have something to think about other than Michael. It was a waste of time and not at all healthy to dwell on those last tense months, the final unhappy weeks that had prompted her to pack her bags and move out. In January, it would be a year, at which time she could obtain her divorce.

At first the snow covered the ground in patches, but it wasn't long before it blanketed everything in sight. Maddy could feel the vehicle climbing and the pressure in her ears beginning to build, and knew she was getting closer to her destination. Nevertheless, she drove slowly and took great care with the curves. The Jeep felt heavy on the winding road. She probably could have done with fewer canned goods, not to mention all those heavy library books she carried with her. She imagined herself

reading in front of a roaring fire while her dogs rested at
her feet. She chuckled softly as she tried to imagine her
dogs at her feet. Not a chance. They'd insist on being
right up in the chair with her. At least the roaring-fire,
part of her fantasy would be possible. She'd covered
herself by bringing wood from home, just in case someone had helped themselves to what was stacked in the
small shed behind the cabin.

Finally, after what seemed an eternity, Maddy came
to the turnoff. The snow was blinding by now, but her
windshield wipers worked overtime, so she could see, if
only for a very short distance. She passed a couple of
cabins, both unoccupied.

Maddy shivered. It suddenly occurred to her that she
might be the only one staying on the mountain now that
a winter storm was in full swing. Perhaps she should
have heeded the warning, or at least told somebody
where she was going. She could feel herself growing
tense.

Had it always been so dark in the mountains at
night?

It was at times like this that she wished she'd chosen
a snarling Doberman for a pet instead of two wimpy
dachshunds who were afraid of their own shadows.
They might make good lapdogs, but they weren't worth
a cuss in the protection department.

Maddy spied the cabin straight ahead and was glad
to have the trip behind her. Well, almost. She still had
to unload the car—not an easy task with the snow coming down so hard. Perhaps she'd unpack just the perish-
able food and leave the rest till daylight. Not that
anything was likely to spoil in this weather. All she

really needed was the bag of dog food. She'd build a fire, soak in a hot bath, maybe read for an hour, and call it a night.

Maddy struggled to stay in the center of the road, but it was impossible to determine exactly where the center was, since there were no tracks. Obviously, it had been snowing for some time in the higher elevations. She crept along, watching for where the road curved into an S. She tried to make out a pattern from the way the weeds clumped together along the side of the road, but with the night casting everything deep in shadow, and the snow whirling about like a tempest, it was impossible to see. Suddenly her Jeep slid on a patch of ice. Maddy reacted too fast. She slammed on the brakes, causing the Jeep to fishtail.

The dachshunds shot up in a flash and began barking in unison as she frantically fought to stay on the road. She knew there were rules on how to correct a skid, because Michael had preached them to her over and over each time they had made the trip to the cabin. But at the moment she didn't have the first clue how to right the Jeep, and her struggles had the car sliding from side to side like some wild carnival ride. Then she felt the back of the vehicle drop off the road.

The engine died.

The barking grew louder.

Maddy leaned her head down on the wheel and told herself not to cry.


Michael was glad he'd taken the time to put chains on his tires, because the roads were hazardous and the snow blinding. Winter storms of this magnitude usually didn't hit the mountains until the New Year. He hoped other motorists had taken the weatherman's advice. He felt silly now for ignoring it; all he could hope for was that the snow would taper off before too long.

Mother Nature wasn't cooperating, though.

Michael braked as he came to a curve. Warning signs flashed from the side of the highway, and he would have turned around if it hadn't been farther to go back down the mountain than up it. He was surprised the state troopers weren't blocking off roads and turning people away, even those with chains on their tires. He wondered if he was making a huge mistake. As the wind shook his car and whipped the snow into a frenzy, Michael hoped he wouldn't live to regret his decision to get away for a while.

He wasn't going to worry. That's the sort of thing that worked against his blood pressure. Beginning now, he was going to learn to relax. Live for today, let tomorrow take care of itself. It wouldn't be easy, especially for someone like him, who'd learned early in life the importance of planning ahead. Even as a child, he'd known what he wanted out of life. More importantly, he'd known what he *didn't* want: the hand-to-mouth existence his parents had endured for as long as he could remember.

Michael pushed the thoughts aside. There he was, worrying for no reason, when he knew damn good and well it wasn't good for him. He pushed a cassette in the tape player, and the car filled with soothing classical music. He let the music carry him to the top of the mountain. He was feeling lethargic, at peace with himself and the rest of the world by the time he reached the turnoff to the cabin.

That peace and tranquillity was shattered the minute he spied the bright red Jeep Cherokee, with its back tires buried in snow. He didn't have to read the "Fit is Fun" tag on the front to know it belonged to Maddy.

Maddy had never been so cold in her life, despite the layers of blankets piled on the bed and her dogs snuggled on either side, offering all their body heat. She wore a blue-green pajama shirt that had belonged to Michael, but a thorough search of dresser drawers hadn't turned up the bottoms. In fact, there wasn't much left in the way of clothes, and her own things were stranded with her car, at least a thousand yards from the cabin.

She sighed. This was going to be a crummy Thanksgiving after all, crummier even than those she'd known as a child. She wished she could kick Dr. Quigley's behind for suggesting she come there. She could stand a little pity from her friends at the moment.

What if . . . what if it snowed so deep she couldn't reach the Jeep? Lord, the possibility of such a tragedy sent her pulse racing. With only three cans of Vienna sausage—no, two cans now that she'd fed one to the dogs—they wouldn't last long if they couldn't get to the food she'd brought with her.

Her dogs.

She would have to pretend everything was okay. If they suspected she was upset, they would become troubled as well. Poor little Muffin, who was so tiny to begin with, would refuse to eat, and Rambo, devil that he was, would start chewing on the furniture.

She'd have to put on a brave front.

She shivered again and wished she had some wood so she could build a fire. Wasn't it just her luck that the roof of the shed had caved in from all the snow. What wood *was* left was wet and buried beneath an avalanche. She'd managed to pull several logs from the pile, but they'd been soaked through. She couldn't have gotten them to burn with a blowtorch.

Maddy had no choice but to wait until morning to try to make it to her car. She was liable to break her leg out there tonight, and *then* where would she be? Thankfully, there were a couple of pairs of wading boots in the utility room. She figured they'd work just as well in snow as they did water. Until then, the three of them would have to stick close. She huddled more deeply beneath the covers, and her dogs snuggled closer. The furry little beasts hadn't had the least bit of trouble falling asleep, she thought, listening to their snores.

She shouldn't have read that detective magazine, but it was all that was left in the way of reading material. She'd lugged her books home on what she'd thought was her last and final trip to the cabin. Now she was not only cold, she was scared half out of her wits thinking about the so-called Hapless Motorist Rapist she'd read about in the magazine. He appealed to women's charitable natures by pretending there was some great emergency and that he was in desperate need of a phone. He even wore clothes that appeared to be blood-soaked. Once the unsuspecting female let him in, she was his.

Maddy felt about for the metal handle on the fire

poker she'd carried into the bedroom for protection. She might be something of a 'fraidy cat, but she was strong and fit.

No man was going to come inside her cabin unless she invited him. Besides, she didn't have a telephone, so he couldn't very well use that excuse.

Maddy drifted off to sleep, only to be awakened a few minutes later by a noise. Startled, she sat up in bed and listened. Sounded like a car. No, surely not. No one in his right mind would be out on a night like this.

No one in his right mind. Comforting thought.

She scrambled from beneath the blankets while at the same time searching frantically for the poker. It had become tangled in the covers. Her dogs woke, sensing trouble, because they shot out of their burrow, yelping wildly. Maddy tried to hush them, but it was useless. She only wished their barks sounded a little more deadly.

Poker in hand, she stumbled to the window on wobbly legs. Lord, but she was a coward. From now on she wouldn't allow herself to read anything darker than the Sunday comics.

She peered outside. There were headlights shining in the drive. Perhaps it wasn't a deranged killer after all. It might be a state trooper coming to check on her, make sure she was okay. Or maybe it was a rescue unit, carrying food and supplies. Wouldn't a taco salad hit the spot about now? She tried to see past the curtain of snow. As the vehicle drew closer she focused her gaze on the roof of it. A feeling of dread washed over her. There was no siren on top. That could only mean one thing.

It was the killer.

Maddy tried to think, but fear clogged her brain. She could grab the puppies and make a run for it out the back door, but they'd freeze to death in a matter of minutes. Unless they could circle back and head down the road to one of the vacant cabins, where she might find dry firewood. No, that wouldn't work. There was no way she'd be able to carry both dogs and a flashlight down the mountain in all that snow, especially with Rambo, the male, weighing sixteen pounds to Muffin's nine.

The car was just outside now. She'd wasted precious time standing there like a dumb statue and hadn't accomplished a thing. It was time to act. She raced from the room, taking time only to close the door behind her. She heard the dogs scratching and yelping before she cleared the hallway.

Suddenly there was pounding at the door. Maddy froze. Her heart thumped like a big drum. The doorknob rattled. He was trying to break in. She strongly suspected it was a man; women seldom became serial killers. Maddy mustered the courage to move closer. The next sound she heard was a key being inserted into the lock.

Panic seized her.

Wasn't it just her luck, the killer had a key to her cabin.

Quickly now, she flattened herself against the wall beside the door, gripped the poker with both hands, and raised it high over her head.

The lock clicked, and the door swung open, creaking like something out of a horror movie. The psycho had left his headlights burning, and she could barely make out the silhouette of a tall man with sweeping shoulders. Without a word, he stepped inside. Maddy brought the poker down on his head. She winced as it made contact with his skull. He gasped, staggered away from the door, and fell into the snow.

Maddy was stunned by her own action, her own strength. She'd actually knocked the would-be killer out cold! She didn't have much time for celebration, though, when she realized she now had a new problem. What the heck was she supposed to do with him? She couldn't leave him lying in the snow; he'd freeze to death in no time. She'd have to drag him in and tie him up until she found out why he had sneaked in on a defenseless woman during a snowstorm.

Hands trembling, she fumbled for the light switch and flipped it on. The light fell across the man's face. Maddy froze at the sight. Everything in her body seemed to shut down. The color drained from her cheeks, her jaw dropped open. Michael? She leaned over the body, and she could almost swear she heard her knees knocking. It was him all right, her soon-to-be ex-husband. She searched for signs of blood. As hard as she'd hit him, she expected to find it gushing from his skull and staining the snow a bright red. She was relieved when she didn't find any; in fact, he looked much the same as he always had, except that he'd put on a few pounds.

Yes, it was definitely Michael.

What the hell was *he* doing *there*? Trying to ruin her chances for a relaxing holiday, no doubt. She'd had to *beg* him to come with her in the past.

He probably wasn't even hurt; just playing possum so she'd feel sorry for him.

Well, he was wasting his time.

With a snort of disgust, she stepped inside the cabin once more, slammed the door, and locked it.

# THREE

Maddy leaned against the door and shook her head. No, this wouldn't do. She couldn't leave Michael out in the snow, even if she did hate him. Sure, she'd told him to drop dead a number of times when their marriage had crumbled, but she had no desire to be responsible for his demise.

Of course, he would probably want to do *her* in when he woke up and found a lump on his head.

A thought nagged her. What if he really *was* hurt? Just because there wasn't any blood didn't mean he wasn't seriously injured. He could be hemorrhaging inside his skull, which was even more dangerous than external bleeding. What if he was out there dying in the snow this very instant? She reached for the doorknob just as someone knocked.

She jumped back, startled at first. So, he wasn't hurt after all, the dirty snake. He'd probably pretended to be, just to frighten her. She had an urge to hit him with the poker again.

Gritting her teeth, she jerked the door open. She blinked several times as she looked into the face of her thirteen-year-old nephew. He looked angry. "Danny?"

"Why'd you hit Uncle Michael?" he demanded.

"Well, I, uh, thought he was a burglar," she sputtered.

"You were going to leave him out here in the snow?"

Maddy blushed. "No. I was just about to open the door when you knocked. Adults sometimes do ridiculous things when they're mad or hurt, Danny. Would you please help me get him in?"

The boy struggled to get his arms beneath those of the unconscious man. Maddy grabbed Michael's legs. "Ready?"

"He's too heavy," Danny said. "You're going to have to pull him."

Maddy pulled with all her might. Several minutes later they had him inside. Danny closed the door while she grabbed a throw pillow from the sofa and tucked it beneath Michael's head. "What are the two of you doing here? And in the middle of a snowstorm to boot?"

Danny didn't seem to be listening. "Why's it so cold in here?" he asked, glancing at the empty fireplace.

"The wood is wet. Please go to the bedroom and get a couple of blankets off the bed." The boy started down the hall. "Don't let the dogs out," she called out.

"Dogs?"

Maddy didn't feel like explaining. "They won't bite."

Danny hurried to do as she asked. Maddy grabbed a flashlight from the kitchen counter and proceeded to check Michael's eyes, lifting each lid and shining the light directly into them. She was vaguely aware of her dogs barking and Danny trying to calm them. Michael's eyes appeared normal. Next, she very gently slid her fingers through his thick, sooty hair. His father had often joked that Michael must've been the product of a sweet-talking milkman; his youngest was the only one who hadn't inherited his father's red hair.

As Maddy searched for a wound she tried not to notice how thick and silky her husband's hair felt between her fingers or the clean scent of his aftershave. He was still as handsome as ever; his face somehow managed to appear both noble and roguish at the same time. She had decided a long time ago that he was lucky to have his olive complexion, since he spent so much time cooped up in an office. He could spend all day in the sun and never burn; she had only to cross the street on a sunny day to get fried.

Maddy sucked her breath in sharply when her fingers located a lump on the back of his head. Oh, Lord, what could she have been thinking?

Danny arrived with the blankets. "Is he hurt bad?"

"I'm not sure There's a big lump, but I don't see an open wound."

"That's good, isn't it?"

Maddy saw the worry on her nephew's face and felt bad for putting it there. She had always been especially fond of the boy. She wished she could ease his mind. "I won't know for a while," she said.

"I thought you knew about injuries and that kind of stuff."

"My specialty is sports injuries, Danny. I know very little about head wounds." She sighed and wished this night had never happened. "He really needs to go to the emergency room, but it's too dangerous to try to find help in this blizzard. Once it's light, I'll try to make it to one of the cabins down the road and see if there's a phone."

Maddy shook her head, feeling dazed as she considered all that had happened in the last ten minutes. Never in a million years would she have guessed she'd run into Michael at their mountain cabin. She'd had to nag him for weeks to buy it; afterward, he'd always had an excuse not to come there.

"Why don't you cover him with that blanket while I get some ice?" she suggested.

When Maddy returned with her homemade ice pack, she found Danny gazing down at his uncle sorrowfully. "Is he going to die?" the boy asked.

Maddy tried to swallow the guilt that rose in the back of her throat, but it refused to go away. "No, of course not," she said. "Once I get the swelling down, it'll be better." She didn't know that for sure—there could be swelling inside Michael's skull, which was more dangerous than any bruise—but she didn't want to frighten her nephew. She was scared enough for both of them.

Maddy placed the ice against the injury. She had a sudden thought. "Wait a minute. I'll bet Michael has his cellular with him."

"Nope." Danny shook his head. "I heard him telling Grandma he was leaving the rat race behind, which he said included his phone and briefcase. That's what the doctor ordered."

She frowned. "What doctor?"

"The one that told him he had high blood pressure. He's supposed to go on a diet and stop smoking."

"Your uncle doesn't smoke, Danny," she said.

"Wanna bet? There was a smoke cloud in his car all the way up here. I could barely breathe."

Maddy was surprised. Michael was very particular about his car; she'd never known him to let anyone smoke in it. She studied her husband closely. She could see he'd gained weight. He'd always been lean and fit, thanks to a steady regimen of jogging She knew how hectic his schedule was; she suspected he was living off junk food these days. No doubt he'd picked up a few other bad habits as well.

"You should have told him the smoke was bothering you, Danny," she said.

"He didn't know I was in the car." The boy stopped abruptly, and it was obvious from his reddening face that he'd said something he shouldn't have.

Maddy gazed back at him. "How could he not know you were in the car?"

Danny looked away quickly. "I was hiding on the floor in the back."

"You were running away from home? I'll bet your poor parents are worried sick."

"I left a note. They know I'm with Uncle Michael. But I plan to split once the roads clear."

"Well, Danny, you're not a baby anymore. I guess there comes a time when a man's got to make his own decisions. I just hope you're prepared." She saw the blank look on his face. "You know, in case some lunatic tries something funny with you. I mean, what kind of people pick up hitchhikers nowadays?"

The boy looked startled at the thought. He opened his mouth to answer but was cut off abruptly when the man on the floor moaned softly.

Maddy snatched her hand away at the sound. Her fingers had grown numb, but she barely noticed. "Michael? Can you hear me?" She could feel her heart thumping wildly in her chest. "Michael? Are you in pain?"

" 'Course he's in pain," Danny said. "You tried to kill him."

Maddy shot the boy a dark look. "Michael, please wake up!" she cried.

"You better hope he doesn't file charges against you for assault and battery."

"This is nothing compared to what I do to mouthy teenagers," Maddy snapped. "Now put a sock in it."

Danny suddenly became quiet.

The man had grown still again, and Maddy feared he would never wake up this time. She shook him gently. "Michael? You need to wake up," she said firmly. Even as she said it she realized just how much she dreaded coming face-to-face with him again. Nevertheless, she had to do what was best for him. She reached out and tugged one earlobe. "Michael, wake up this minute!" she said sharply.

"Hey, what do you think you're doing?" Danny protested.

"I'm trying to provoke him. He hates having his ears touched."

"Oh, I get it." Danny leaned close. "Open your eyes, Mike!" he shouted so loud that Maddy thought she'd jump out of her skin. "He hates being called

Mike." The man on the floor shifted and frowned. "See, it's working."

"Oh, Michael," Maddy said dramatically. "Ernest Tate has gone and made Brenner full partner. You know how much you dislike Adam Brenner. He's going to eat your lunch, Michael. You're going to end up working for him."

"You're a crappy attorney anyway, Mike," Danny said, his voice ringing off the cabin walls. "A real slug. You couldn't win a case if your life depended on it."

Michael's eyes twitched and fluttered open. He blinked once or twice as if to focus. Maddy breathed a sigh of relief as consciousness began to register on his face.

Danny was gazing at the ceiling as if looking for inspiration. He was beginning to like this game. "Man, you ain't got squat for brains, Mike. You could put your brains on the head of a pin, and you'd still have room to park your car. And how 'bout your mama? Why she's so ugly, she has to sneak up on a glass to get a drink of water."

Maddy noted the dark look on Michael's face. "That's enough, Danny," she said.

"I'm talking ugly," Danny said. "Your mama's so ugly she has to—" With lightning speed, the man reached up and grasped the boy by the collar of his shirt. Danny shrieked and made a gagging sound. "Aunt Maddy, he's choking me! Make him let go."

"Michael, no!" Maddy tried to pull the boy free, but she was no match for the man. Danny gagged. His face was the color of fresh strawberries. "You're hurting him, Michael!" she cried. "He's just a kid. Let him go."

Michael blinked several times as though trying to understand what she was saying. Finally, he released Danny. The boy coughed and sputtered, then glared at his aunt and uncle. "Man, you guys are crazy, you know that?" He leaped to his feet. "I'm almost sorry I left home." He stormed off toward the bedroom.

Maddy jumped when the door slammed. She knew she was going to have to apologize, but first she had to see to Michael. He was staring at her with a strange look on his face.

"Why am I lying on the floor?" he said.

"You, uh, fell," she said. "You have a big knot on your head." She decided not to tell him the truth until he was better. "I need to put more ice on it. Do you think you can sit up?"

Very slowly, he pushed himself into an upright position. He felt the back of his head and winced when he discovered the lump. The pain seemed to radiate through his skull. "Do you have any aspirin?"

"Yes, of course. Let me help you up, and I'll get it." Holding one of his arms, she struggled to get him to his feet. He swayed, and she grabbed him around his waist to steady him. He felt familiar, despite the added pounds. When he looked as though he could stand on his own, she went into the kitchen and grabbed the aspirin bottle and a glass of water. She turned and discovered he was watching her.

"Are you okay?" she asked.

He just stared at her.

He was beginning to frighten her. But that was ridiculous; they had lived together for five years, had known each other almost seven. "Here, you'll feel better after you take this." Maddy shook two aspirin into his palm and handed him the water.

"Thanks." Michael popped the aspirin into his mouth and drank all the water before returning the glass. He took in his surroundings, the plaid sofa and chair with plump cushions, the dried-flower arrangement, and the matted and framed photographs that hung on the wall. The empty fireplace made him frown. "It's freezing in here. You should have a fire going."

Maddy wondered at his impersonal tone. He'd obviously been very successful at shutting her out of his life; she almost hated herself for the buckets of tears she'd cried after leaving him. "The wood is wet, Michael," she said. "I carried in a couple of loads, but it's going to take a while for them to dry out." His gaze landed on her once more. "I'd better find that ice pack. The sooner we get that swelling down the better." She started for the kitchen, then paused. "Would you like something? A cup of coffee or some hot chocolate. We don't have much water, so we'll have to conserve as much as we can until we find the water valve."

"Huh?"

He looked at her as though she'd just rattled the whole thing off in German. Maybe he was still dazed. In that case, she wouldn't want to give him more to think about than he needed at the moment. "I asked whether I could get you anything," she said.

"Some answers would be nice," he said sharply. "For starters, I'd like to know where the hell I am. Once you answer that, you might tell me who *you* are."

# FOUR

Maddy was too stunned at first to speak. "You're saying you don't know who I am? Is this some kind of joke?"

"Do I look like I'm joking?"

She had to admit he didn't. His eyes were dark and hooded, impenetrable. There was an aloofness about him that made her edgy. His body language told her he was as tense with the situation as she was. She didn't like what she was thinking. Surely to heaven he didn't have amnesia. Those things only happened on TV, not in real life. "No, you don't."

The bedroom door opened and two dachshunds raced out, going into a fit of barking the minute they spied Michael. They skidded to a stop and attached themselves to the hem of his jeans, growling and snarling as though they had every intention of tearing them off his body.

Danny followed close behind. He looked hurt and embarrassed. "I'm sorry I said those things about Grandma, Uncle Michael," he said, trying to make himself heard over the noise. Maddy was on her knees trying to pull the animals free. "I was just trying to get you to wake up. I'm glad you're okay." Without warning, he threw his arms around Michael.

Maddy managed to pry Muffin loose, but Rambo refused to give up, dodging all her attempts to grab him. She would have to close the female in her bedroom, then try to wrestle the male free. She stood, and noted the frantic look on Michael's face. He obviously didn't know what to make of the boy.

"Uh, Danny, I have something to tell you," Maddy began, struggling to hold her pet, who seemed bent on diving from her arms and rejoining her brother.

As though sensing a problem, the boy drew back and looked into his uncle's face. "Is something wrong, Uncle Michael?"

"Your uncle doesn't recognize us, honey. He has amnesia."

Danny looked from one to the other. "Is this for real or are you guys being weird again?"

Michael, who was trying to pull free from the animal's grasp, glanced up. "It must be real because I don't have a clue what's going on here."

"What *do* you remember?" the boy asked.

"Well . . ." Michael took a few steps into the living room, dragging the dachshund as he went. He heard the sound of denim ripping, and he hoped he hadn't paid a lot for the jeans. He had a sudden urge to toss the dog out in the snow, but the woman grabbed the mutt before he could act on it.

"I'm so sorry," Maddy said, wondering what had turned her pets into beasts. They obviously sensed Michael wasn't an animal lover. Still, that was no excuse. She carried them down the hall, one tucked beneath each arm. Their tails wagged excitedly, slapping against her back as she fussed. "You two can forget having any T-R-E-A-T-S today," she said, spelling out the word because she didn't want them to become more excited than they were. She set them down inside the bedroom and ignored their sad-eyed expression as she pulled on the jeans and sneakers she'd worn on the drive up. "Go to sleep," she ordered the dogs, and closed the door. She found Michael sitting on the sofa when she returned to the living room. "Have you remembered anything?"

He looked at her. "I remember waking up this morning and going to work," he said. "I know I'm a lawyer. I don't know *how* I know, but I do. That's about it. Look, it's really cold in here. Why don't I get some firewood out of my trunk?"

"You have wood in your trunk!"

He suddenly looked baffled. "Gee, I don't know. I must. Otherwise, why would I have said it? I guess the only way to find out is to check." He stood.

"Oh, no, you don't," Maddy told him. "Give me the keys to your car, and Danny and I will look. You need to sit down and put this ice pack on your head."

Michael reached into his pocket for his car keys and handed them to her. He took the ice pack and placed it against his head. It hurt like a son-of-a-gun. "You never did tell me who you are."

"She's the one who tried to kill you," Danny said. He was still smarting from being called a kid. "I saw it with my own two eyes. She 'bout knocked your brains out."

Maddy felt the heat rush to her cheeks. "Danny!"

Michael touched the back of his head and winced. It was sore as hell. "What did you hit me with, a sledge-hammer?"

Danny grabbed the poker from the floor. "She hit you with this," he said. "Then, when you fell into the snow, she slammed the door and locked you out. You would have died out there if I hadn't banged on the door and made her bring you inside."

"That's enough, young man!" Maddy snapped, taking the poker from him. Her thunderous expression must have convinced him she meant what she said, because he buttoned his lip tight.

"I hope you had a very good reason for hitting me," Michael said, his lips pressed into a grim line.

She didn't quite meet his gaze. "I thought you were going to hurt me."

"Do I have a history of violence?"

"No. It's just, well, you were coming in the door so fast, and it was dark."

"Perhaps next time you'll try to get a better look before you risk crushing an innocent person's skull."

He was using his lawyer's voice now. "If I acted too hastily, it was because I was afraid," she said. "You can't imagine what it's like up here all alone."

"Perhaps you should stay home where you feel safe," he replied.

She gave him a biting smile. "And perhaps you should identify yourself when you're entering a dark cabin in the middle of nowhere. The next person you run into might have a gun."

Maddy left both of them long enough to retrieve the wading boots, mismatched gloves, and various knitted caps from the utility room. She handed Danny what he'd need. When he looked incredulous at the pink knitted scarf he held, she insisted. "Don't give me a hard time. We can't afford to get sick."

"Oh, yes," Michael said. "We certainly can't risk a head cold, can we? Brain injuries, on the other hand, are okay."

Maddy gritted her teeth as she pulled the boots and gloves on. He was very definitely getting on her nerves. She planted her hands on her hips and glared at him. "Look, it was dark, I was scared, so I defended myself. Okay?"

Still holding the ice pack against his head, Michael stood. "To say you were defending yourself is to imply I was trying to do you bodily harm. I seriously doubt that was the case."

"I made a mistake," she almost shouted. "Are we going to rehash it until we freeze to death? I'm sorry. What more can I say?"

"You can answer my question," he replied. "Who the hell are you?"

Danny, who'd already booted up, was trying to pull on a pair of ladies' gloves. He glanced up, looked from one to the other, and spoke. "She's your wife, Uncle Michael."

Maddy had the distinct pleasure of watching the man pale before her very eyes. "Happy now?" she asked. He slumped onto the sofa in a daze. "Try not to look so miserable," she told him. "We're in the process of a divorce." She motioned for her nephew. "Come on, Danny."

Maddy and Danny stepped out into the blizzard. The force of the wind was so strong, they could barely walk. Luckily, Michael had parked his car close. Maddy was still smarting from the look Michael had given her when he'd learned they were man and wife. As if there was something wrong with her! Well, he didn't have to worry about *that* much longer. In a couple of more months he'd be a free agent.

Maddy pushed her thoughts aside and unlocked the trunk. What she found there lifted her spirits. Firewood. Enough to last several days, even if they burned it around the clock. That would give her ample time to get to her supply in the Jeep.

"Wow!" Danny said through chattering teeth.

"Hold your arms out, and I'll give you a stack." For once, he did what she said without arguing. They each grabbed as much as they could hold and carried it to the cabin door. Michael was waiting for them. He'd donned cap and gloves as well.

"I see you found some wood." He took several logs from her to lighten her load.

"Your trunk is almost full," Maddy said as she and Danny stepped inside. "There's a bunch of it. Why aren't you resting? And where's the ice pack?"

Michael took the wood from her. "First things first. We need to get as much firewood in here as we can in case this storm gets worse, which it probably will." He carried the wood over to the fireplace and set it down, then grabbed Danny's load. After stacking it near the hearth, he looked at Maddy. "Can you build a good fire?"

"Of course I can." If he could remember anything, he would know that she was better at it than he was.

"Okay, while you do that Danny and I will bring in the rest of the wood."

The boy looked pleased to be included in what was obviously turning into a man's job.

Maddy started to protest, but she knew it was hopeless. She went to work, stacking wood on the grate, stuffing old newspapers beneath it. In ten minutes' time the wood had been unloaded and Maddy had a roaring fire going. They stood around it, letting the heat chase the chill from their bodies.

"Are you up to helping me unload the rest of the car?" Michael asked Danny.

The boy nodded bravely, and they went to work once more. Maddy dumped more ice cubes into a sauce pan and set it on the stove to melt. She was thankful when Michael finally closed the cabin door and locked it.

"Is there anything decent to eat?" Danny called out, warming his hands at the fire.

Maddy chuckled. Her mood had improved dramatically now that they had supplies, although she admitted it would be nice to have running water. "Sorry, Danny, your uncle only brought bad food. Do you like brussels sprouts?" She glanced at him, saw that he'd taken her seriously. "Just kidding. I'm putting together a snack right now."

Danny dove into the plate of cold cuts when she carried them into the living room. Maddy and Michael exchanged amused looks. "I have instant coffee," she said, glad to see he was sitting down and using the ice pack. "Would you like a cup?"

"Yeah, thanks."

"I'll take some too," Danny told her.

Maddy knew Brenda wouldn't go for that at all. "Sorry, kiddo. You're getting hot chocolate." She returned to the kitchen, prepared the hot beverages, and carried them into the living room on a wooden tray.

"I forgot to tell you I take a spoon of sugar in mine," Michael said once she set the tray down.

"Yes, I know."

"That's right, you would know, wouldn't you? Sorry, I forgot." He shrugged. "What am I talking about, I've forgotten everything."

"It's probably temporary."

"Let's hope so. I still have to earn a living. It won't look good if I get back to work and don't remember my clients' names. Or how to do my job," he added bitterly.

Maddy didn't have an answer for that one. He was never going to forgive her for hitting him over the head, and she really couldn't blame her. She should have waited to get a better look before slamming him. But there wasn't a darn thing she could do about it now. The damage was done, and she refused to feel guilty over it. She sat on the sofa and sipped her coffee in silence.

Holding the ice pack in one hand and his coffee cup in the other, Michael studied her. As worried as he was over his condition, he knew it was unfair to blame her for trying to defend herself. She had obviously been very frightened at the time.

"I believe I heard Danny call you Maddy," he said, trying to strike up a conversation with her.

She glanced at him. Some of the tension had left his face. She wondered if he'd gotten over being mad. "It's short for Madison. I was named after my grandfather."

"Why are we divorcing?" he asked.

"It's very complicated," she said. "I don't think this is the right time to discuss it."

"I wasn't having an affair, was I?"

Danny chuckled but didn't say anything.

The question caught her by surprise. "I wasn't aware of an affair. Why do you ask?"

Michael shrugged. "You're a beautiful woman. I can't imagine any man cheating on you."

"Thank you," she said stiffly. Maddy grabbed a piece of cheese and nibbled on it. The fire was making her drowsy, but she knew she couldn't go to sleep. She'd have to sit up with Michael. She excused herself and tiptoed down the hall to the bedroom. Her dachshunds were huddled together at the foot of the bed, both asleep. She left the door open so the heat could get in. She returned to the living room and tucked a couple of blankets around Danny, who was dozing in front of the fire.

"How come there's no heating device here?" Michael asked.

Maddy was thankful for the change of subject as she reclaimed her seat on the sofa. "The cabin was very primitive when we bought it a couple of years back. It had electricity and inside plumbing, but that was about it. You were talking to someone about installing heaters when we put it on the market."

"Whose idea was it to sell the place?"

Maddy took a sip of her coffee. "Mine."

"Because of the divorce?"

"Yes. I was crazy for suggesting we buy it in the first place, what with the hours you work." He lifted one dark brow. "You usually put in seventy-to-eighty-hour work weeks," she said.

"Are you divorcing me because I work too many hours?"

"I'm afraid there was more to it than that."

Danny shifted on the floor and opened his eyes. "Do you have a pillow?"

"You can sleep on the bed," Maddy told him. "Uncle Michael and I will probably stay up for a while because of his head injury." Without a word, the boy got up and stumbled down the hall toward the bedroom.

"You don't have to sit up with me," Michael said.

"Of course I do. After all, *I* caused your injury."

He managed a small smile. "I'm sorry for giving you a hard time. You obviously felt threatened or you wouldn't have done it." He paused, and his smile faded as another thought hit him. "Unless you really *did* know who I was, and you were trying to pay me back for being a crummy husband."

Maddy noted, with amusement, the worried look in his eyes. "You weren't *that* crummy. At least not enough for me to try to kill you," she added.

He didn't look happy. "You make me sound like an ogre. Was I?"

"We're too different, that's all."

"Didn't we know this before we married?"

"I think we were too much in love at the time. I remember thinking I could change you. That was my mistake, not yours. Don't worry, you'll have your memory back soon," she said, sounding more confident than she felt.

"Until then, I'll just have to wait for my information. Is that it?"

Maddy realized he'd been holding the ice pack against his head longer than he should have. She stood. "You'd better take a break from the ice," she said, knowing it was best to leave it on only ten minutes at a time. "Let me check the bump." She leaned over and examined him.

Michael wasn't prepared for her closeness or the smell of her perfume. His gut tightened.

"I don't know if it's my imagination or if the lump has actually grown smaller," she said. "Does it still hurt?"

He was hurting, all right, but it had nothing to do with his head. "It's okay," he said, his voice strained.

Maddy took the ice pack from him. "I'd offer you more coffee, but I'm afraid we're low on ice cubes, and we really need them for your head."

He stared at her. "I know there's logic in there somewhere, I just haven't found it yet."

Once again, she explained the situation about the water valve.

"Go ahead and use the ice cubes. I'll see if I can find the water valve in the morning," he said. "Am I really not supposed to go to sleep?"

"It's not a good idea after you've had a serious head

injury." She saw the weary expression on his face and felt bad. He'd probably had to put in a lot of hours to obtain time off, and now he couldn't get the rest he needed.

Maddy carried the cups to the kitchen and refilled them. She heard Michael stoking the fire, and when she glanced over her shoulder, she saw him drop another log on. He flipped on the light switch beside the sliding-glass door and pulled the drapes open on each side.

"It's really coming down out there," he said.

She carried the cups into the living room and gazed out at the sight. The only time she'd seen it snow so hard was at her parents' home on Martha's Vineyard. "Looks like we both picked a perfect place to spend Thanksgiving," she said.

He checked the date on his wristwatch. "That's right, it *is* Thanksgiving, isn't it?" He took his cup from her and sipped his coffee in silence as he watched the snow fall. "Well, we've got everything here we need. A roof over our heads and enough food to keep us for a while." He returned his gaze to the window. "I guess that has to be the most spectacular thing I've ever seen," he confessed.

Maddy thought it was an odd thing for him to say. The Michael she knew wouldn't waste time gazing out at a snowstorm; he'd be trying to figure a way to escape. Nor would he be content to sit in front of the fire with her, sipping coffee and talking about inane topics. For most of their five years together she'd dined alone each night and later climbed into an empty bed. Once in a while, usually out of guilt, Michael would come home early. They'd have dinner together, and she would clean up while he showered. They would make love, and for an hour or so Maddy would be convinced everything was going to be okay. Michael had always been a thoughtful lover, and it was during those times that she told herself she could forgive him everything else.

Afterward, she'd lie in his arms and try to talk to him, but she could feel him growing restless. She knew each time his eyes darted to the alarm clock, knew he was trying to make a graceful exit. Once he was gone, Maddy was left to fall asleep alone as usual. It had been a lonely existence, which would have been more tolerable had they had children. But Michael didn't want children, a fact he'd hammered home when she'd become pregnant.

"You look a million miles away," Michael said, breaking into her thoughts. "Want to talk about it?"

The sound of his voice startled her, and she looked up. His gaze was penetrating, and she half feared he knew everything she'd been thinking. "I need to check to see if the bedroom is warm enough," she said, getting up quickly. She started down the hall, thankful to have something to do.

Maddy stepped into the bedroom. From the light in the hall, she saw that her nephew was tucked beneath the covers. The small humps on either side of him told her the dogs were snuggled close.

She tiptoed out of the room and made her way into the kitchen, where she set the dishes in the sink and wiped down the counters. She glanced over at Michael, who was staring into the fire, his brow wrinkled as though deep in thought. She wondered if he was trying to remember.

What would he have to say once his memory came back? *If* it came back. She didn't know which she feared most, his memory never returning or him getting it back full force and remembering all that had transpired between them.

"Anything I can help with?" Michael asked.

Maddy jumped at the sound of his voice. Damned if the man didn't move as quietly as a cat. "I'm finished," she said, draping the wet dishcloth over a metal rack beside the sink. She started out of the kitchen, but he blocked her way. "Excuse me," she said. "I'd like to get by."

"Not so fast. I just thought of something." He stepped closer, placed his hands on either side of her shoulders, and dipped his head.

Maddy was jolted to her toes when his lips touched hers. Once she could think clearly, she tried to pull away. Instead of letting her go, he grasped her around the waist and pulled her closer. He broke the kiss and pressed his lips against her throat.

"Michael?" Maddy could hear the catch in her voice. "Please stop."

He moved his lips to an earlobe and nibbled it. He felt her shiver, then realized she was trembling. He glanced up. His ardor died at the sight of her tears. He released her and stepped back. "I'm sorry," he said. "I thought—"

"What did you think?" she asked coolly. "That I might provide a diversion for you, alleviate your boredom a little while since there's nothing else to do?"

He looked offended. "Not at all. I thought, well, I'd hoped that I might remember something if I, if we . . ." He paused. "I'm sorry to have imposed on you." He left the kitchen and returned to the living room, where he put another log on the fire.

Maddy busied herself with unnecessary chores in the kitchen until she saw that he was absorbed in a book. Finally, she crept into the living room, grabbed a blanket, and sat on the sofa. She almost laughed out loud when she saw that Michael was reading a Tom Clancy novel. He wouldn't last through the first chapter, she thought. He was forced to do so much reading at work that he no longer did it for pleasure. So why was he reading a book now?

He glanced up at her as though she'd asked the question out loud. "Why are you staring at me?"

"I'm not used to seeing you read a book."

"I enjoy reading." He paused. "Don't I?"

"At one time you did. We used to swap books when we were dating. Later you didn't have time." Maddy lay back on the sofa and snuggled beneath the blankets, feeling warm and cozy as she gazed into the fire and listened to the logs snap and hiss. Her eyes burned from fatigue, and her lids drooped. One yawn led to another. Finally, she could no longer resist closing her eyes.

Michael closed the book he was reading and leaned his head back against the chair, wincing when he accidentally bumped the knot on his head. He touched it lightly. The swelling had gone down, but his head still ached something fierce. He watched Maddy as she slept. She was, without a doubt, the loveliest creature he'd ever seen, and he couldn't believe he didn't remember her.

He wondered what he'd done to make her want to

divorce him, and he suspected whatever it was, it had to have been bad.

When Michael opened his eyes the next morning, his head felt as though someone had dribbled it across a concrete basketball court. The lump was still sore as all get-out. Not only that, he was shivering. The fire had died out, and the cabin had grown cold again. He glanced at Maddy on the sofa and found both dachshunds snuggled against her. They'd obviously searched for her during the night.

Michael checked his wristwatch and was surprised to find it was after ten o'clock. Very quietly, he stood and walked to the sliding-glass door and pulled back the curtain. It looked as though the storm had dumped a good eighteen inches of snow on the ground, and it was still coming down. No telling how bad the roads were or how long it would be before they were cleared.

A thought suddenly occurred to him. He couldn't have planned it more perfectly. After fruitless months of trying to reach Maddy at work or find out where she lived, it had taken a storm to bring them face-to-face again. She would have no choice but to listen to what he had to say now.

And he had plenty.

Such as how he'd screwed up by not putting her first in his life.

And how he would do anything, even quit his job if he had to, to win her back.

He would even reconsider having children, if it meant that much to her.

Michael was jolted by the thoughts racing through his brain. Where were they coming from? What had happened to the brick wall that had blocked so much of his past until this very moment? Now he was bombarded with memories.

He gazed at the lovely creature on the sofa and agonized that she had been a stranger to him for several hours the night before. How was that possible when he still loved her more than life itself?

Michael felt like rejoicing at the second chance he'd been given, but he knew he had a lot of work to do.

# FIVE

Michael didn't have long to celebrate his good fortune before he wondered what he was going to do about it. He had a feeling that Maddy wasn't likely to be as pleased as he was about regaining his memory. Until now, she had treated him with a certain amount of politeness. Once she discovered the real Michael Kelly was back in residence, she was liable to hit him over the head again with the poker, then lock herself and her pets in the bedroom till the roads cleared.

No, he couldn't tell her yet. Not until he proved he'd changed into the kind of husband she'd be proud of.

She certainly wouldn't sit still and listen as he told her what a jerk he'd been. She already knew he was a jerk.

He hadn't even realized how much he loved her until it was too late. Until she'd lost their baby and moved out.

No wonder she hated him.

Jerk was too kind a word to describe his behavior.

Michael heard her moan softly in her sleep, and the dachshunds instantly awoke, gazing at their mistress with open adoration. And why not? She was the epitome of sweetness and kindness, and he had taken her for granted. Even his family adored her. They'd suffered almost as much as he had when she'd left him.

She awoke by degrees, and Michael was reminded of a rose blossoming under time-lapse photography. Her face was flushed, and her thick hair fell against her cheek like a caress. He wished he could bury his face in that hair and inhale her scent or slide his hands inside her clothes and touch her warm, smooth skin. At one time she would have welcomed it; now he worried that he might never have that opportunity again.

She had done everything possible to avoid him since their separation—moving to an undisclosed location, getting an unlisted phone number, having her mail sent to a post-office box. He'd gone by the gym where she worked a couple of times, but two muscle-bound goons whom he referred to as Dumber and Dumbest, had escorted him out as soon as he set foot in the place. He'd been in the process of brainstorming a new strategy when her attorney had him served with divorce papers and a restraining order.

It was clear she'd meant business. He couldn't even sit in the parking lot and gaze at her from a distance or he'd be arrested. Had it not been for his job, he might have risked it.

Of course, he'd had ample opportunities to look at her during their five years of marriage. But he'd been too damn busy and consumed with his career.

Jerk.

Maybe this time he'd get it right. He would show her he was a different man. He would sweep her off her feet, he would— He frowned. Danny. Why had Maddy brought him? It wasn't going to be easy to romance his wife with a thirteen-year-old boy watching his every move.

Maddy opened her eyes and found herself looking into Michael's handsome face. At first she was confused. Suddenly it all came back to her.

"Good morning," Michael said, startling her dogs, who immediately went into a barking frenzy. She reached for them but was a second too late. They went straight for the hem of his jeans. When she started to get up, he stopped her. "Don't worry, they're not bothering me."

"They'll ruin your jeans."

"These old things? Nah. Besides, I like dogs." He noted her look of disbelief as he leaned over to pet the larger dachshund, the male. The dog gave a menacing snarl and sank his teeth into Michael's thumb.

"Rambo, no!" Maddy cried, practically leaping from the sofa. The dogs saw her coming after them and ran behind the chair. It was obvious they were unaccustomed to being scolded by their mistress. "Oh, I'm *so* sorry!" she said, taking Michael's hand in hers so she could get a better look at the wound. "I don't know what's gotten into them, they've *never* acted like this. And Rambo is so good-natured," she said. As if to prove her assertion, the male dog wagged his tail frantically, and it thumped against the wall. "He's had his rabies shots, by the way."

Michael was only vaguely aware of the words coming out of Maddy's mouth. With her holding his hand, and her blonde head bent over it, he could smell the fragrance of her shampoo. It was a clean scent, making him think of things like freshly laundered towels or the way everything smelled after a spring shower. He closed his eyes.

"I need to clean it," she said.

"Don't worry about it," he said, putting on a brave face. "I'm used to this sort of thing. Happens all the time."

She stepped back, looking alarmed. "You're used to getting bit by dogs?"

Michael noticed the blood was beginning to ooze steadily, but the last thing he wanted to do was make a big deal out of it and let her think he was a wimp. He pinched the wound with his other finger, hoping the pressure would stop the bleeding. It hurt like the dickens. "What I meant was, I get my share of cuts and scrapes, and it's no big deal."

"Michael, there's blood dripping on your pants, for heaven's sake!" She grabbed his other hand and pulled him into the kitchen. "Hold it over the sink while I get the first-aid kit." She hurried into the bathroom.

As he watched her go, all in a flurry, Michael couldn't help but wonder if her concern was out of some leftover feelings for him. No, she probably felt guilty because it was her dog that bit him. As if acting on cue, both dachshunds came into the kitchen. Rambo growled; Michael growled in reply. They both yelped and ran from the room as Maddy entered.

"What happened?" she asked, a worried look in her eyes. "I heard the pups cry out."

Pretending to study his thumb at the sink, Michael glanced up. "Huh? I didn't hear anything." Glancing into the living room, he experienced a wicked sense of pleasure at finding the dogs in their hiding place behind the chair. "Maybe they saw a mouse," he said, then wished he hadn't as soon as he remembered Maddy was terrified of mice.

"A mouse? Oh, no, I didn't think of that. There should be traps in the utility room. Only—" She paused and swallowed.

"Only what?"

"If one gets trapped, I don't think I could, you know." She shivered.

"I'll take care of it, Maddy."

She blinked several times, caught off guard by the sudden gentleness in his tone. As their gazes met she felt a tiny thrill of excitement run through her. She had learned you could hate a man and be angry enough to kill him, but somehow manage to love him still. That was the part that hurt the most. Which is why she had gone to a lot of trouble to keep from seeing him these past months. Now she realized what a fool she'd been. Love didn't fade away easily.

Nor did the pain. It was as fresh as it had been the day she'd told him she was pregnant and had witnessed the deep disappointment on his face.

Seeing the look on Maddy's face, Michael feared he was, once again, on the verge of being discovered. He had to stop screwing up. "What is it?"

After a moment she shrugged. "You sounded like

your old self for a minute, that's all." She set the first-aid kit on the counter and opened the bottle of peroxide. "Okay, first I'm going to clean it with this. It might sting a bit." She poured it on his finger, then opened the kit and grabbed a square of sterile gauze to dry the wound. "It's not deep," she said, obviously relieved. "I won't have to amputate after all." She reached for a tube of ointment, and a large bandage strip.

"Guess I don't get to collect my sick days, huh?"

She gave a cynical laugh. "The Michael I know wouldn't call in sick if he were missing all ten fingers. Matter of fact, he was in court and couldn't be bothered the day I was in the hospital losing his baby."

Maddy heard his quick intake of breath and realized what she'd said. She regretted the words instantly, but it was too late, they'd already left her mouth. She glanced up quickly, Michael's eyes reflected the pain she felt inside. Tears sprinted to her eyes. She was embarrassed to the point of humiliation. She wanted to go somewhere and hide her face, but she had to see to his injured thumb first. She swallowed hard. "I don't believe I said that."

Michael felt as if she'd struck him, but he knew he deserved it. He had been in court the day she'd miscarried, but his secretary would have gotten word to him in the event of an emergency. Maddy had called, he'd been told during a brief recess, but she hadn't left a message. After the way he'd shut her out, she'd probably assumed he wouldn't come. He'd learned about it from his sister-in-law Brenda, but when he'd finally arrived at the hospital, Maddy had asked him to leave. She'd packed her

bags and moved out the next day as he was giving closing arguments in his case.

"Maybe it needed saying," he replied after a moment.

"I'm not a cruel person."

He gave her a small smile. "One only has to look at
you to know that."

Maddy reached for the ointment and applied it to
the wound. She suddenly felt emotionally fragile and ill-
equipped to handle being closed in with her soon-to-be
ex-husband. But what could she do? With no phone and
no transportation out of there, she had no choice. If
only she could put her emotions aside until it was over.

Michael noted the cloud of unease on Maddy's face,
and he wished there was something he could say or do
to wipe it away, make her feel better. He would have
given his entire education and all that he'd achieved at
Smyth-McGraw to be able to take her in his arms at
that moment and kiss away her fears and doubts. He
longed to tell her the things he'd learned since she'd left
him—how all the money and power in the world didn't
mean a thing if there was no love in your life. He knew
that if his life were to end tomorrow, he'd rather go to
his grave a poor man, who'd known the passion and
tenderness of a woman, than die rich and alone.

But Maddy wasn't ready to hear this. At least not
from him. He had to earn her trust before he could
share those things he'd discovered each time he walked
into their empty condo at the end of the day or reached
out for her in the night, only to remember, with a heavy
heart, that she was gone.

"There now," Maddy said, once she'd put the bandage on his thumb. "You're good to go. Try to keep your fingers away from jealous dachshunds."

"I've been meaning to talk to you about the way you're spoiling those mutts," he said, hoping to chase the shadows from her eyes with a little teasing.

Maddy cleaned up the mess and closed the first-aid kit. "Too late, the damage has been done. And I suggest you stop calling them mutts or Rambo might try to take off something a little more important than just a thumb next time."

This amused him. "Such as?"

Maddy saw the sudden wicked gleam in his eyes and realized her meaning had been misconstrued. Blushing profusely, she quickly chastised herself for not thinking before she spoke. "That's not what I meant."

"Uh-huh."

The heat spread to her ears. She wished he weren't standing so close. And why did he have to look so good, for Pete's sake! Even in wrinkled clothes and a day's growth of whiskers, he looked like he belonged on the cover of some outdoor magazine. "By the way, how's your head this morning?" she asked, deciding a change of subject was exactly what they needed at the moment.

He grinned. It was refreshing to know there were still women who blushed. "Much better, thanks."

"Do you remember anything?"

"I remember packing my car yesterday to come here. Seems I remember driving here. It was a mess, all that snow."

"That's all?"

"I'm sorry."

"You don't have to be sorry. You didn't do anything wrong. I'm just concerned."

He felt hopeful. Surely, her concern had to mean something. "You needn't worry yourself over me," he said.

"Of course I do. I'm the one responsible for your injury."

It wasn't exactly the reason he'd hoped for, but he managed a smile. "I promise I won't file charges against you."

"I'm going to try to make it to the cabins down the road," she said. "To see if there's a telephone. I may have to break in, but I doubt I'll go to jail, under the circumstances."

He resisted the urge to laugh. If she thought for one minute he was going to let her go traipsing off in knee-deep snow, she could think again. But he knew, short of tying her up, she would do as she damn well pleased. Maddy might be prissy in some ways, but she knew her own mind, and she didn't let anyone tell her what to do.

"I don't suppose we ever kept any firearms up here, did we?" He already knew the answer to that. Unlike his brothers on the police force, he wasn't big on guns. The one sport he did permit himself was archery. He'd been very good in college, winning all sorts of awards. He'd brought his bow and arrow with him, hoping a little target practice would relieve some of his stress, but he seriously doubted he'd have to use it for any other reason.

"You never allowed guns in the house," she said. "Why do you ask?"

"I'd feel better if you were armed. You know, with all these critters about."

One brow lifted. "Critters?"

"With the trees bare and the ground covered, I'm afraid we might get a few hungry bears."

"Bears?"

"I'm probably wrong. I'd think most of them would be in hibernation. I just hate to see you take such a chance when the likelihood of finding a phone up here is so slim."

"You know, you're probably right," she said quickly. "Those cabins look very primitive. I doubt they even have electricity, much less a telephone. No telling where we'd have to go to make a call." She suddenly brightened. "I'll bet you have flares in your car."

Michael just looked at her, not knowing if it was something he should remember or not. "I'll have to check. I wouldn't send them up today, though, because of the thick cloud cover. Besides, rescue workers are going to be busy with emergencies." He was trying to buy as much time as he could.

"You don't consider your condition an emergency?"

"My memory will return soon enough," he assured her. He went into the living room and dropped a log on the fire. Her pets jumped to their feet and started barking, but he ignored them.

Maddy shushed the dogs and watched Michael stir the fire. She couldn't believe he could be so casual about his injury. "Danny said you were seeing a doctor for high blood pressure. That probably means you're taking medication. Might be a good idea to look for it." When he didn't answer, she went on. "I'll bet you didn't know you had a stowaway in your car. Danny ran away from home."

Michael was genuinely surprised. He could just imagine what his brother and sister-in-law were going through. "I'll bet his family is having a fine Thanksgiving," he muttered. "Probably worried out of their minds. And no way to call them." He shook his head sadly. He was going to have to hike to a phone after all.

"Danny claims he left a note telling his parents he was going with you. They'll probably be more angry with him than worried." Maddy was craving a cup of coffee in the worst way. She suspected there might be enough ice cubes left to melt and boil the necessary water. She dumped the remaining two ice trays into a pot and turned the gas on low. With that done, she started down the hall, both dachshunds at her feet. She grabbed their litter box from the bedroom, where Danny was still asleep, and moved it to the utility room.

"Go potty," she said to the dogs, who simply stared back at her as though she'd just spouted off something only kitty cats could understand. Rambo ducked his head and wagged his tail, which caused the lower half of his body to move from side to side as though he were doing the hula. Muffin sat up on her hind legs and shivered. Finally, Rambo stepped into the box, did his business, and beamed as Maddy praised him. Her gave her a love bite on her chin and jumped out. Since the box wasn't that big, she had to clean it before Muffin could go.

One thing about being alone all those months, Maddy'd had plenty of time to train her pets properly. When she was at work, they used their litter pan, but once she returned home, she let them run about the property while she watched from her front-porch swing. It gave them a chance to exercise and her a chance to relax. She had purchased several acres so that she didn't have to worry about them getting in the road or bothering anybody. She had several fat cats and a horse as well, which she was paying a neighbor kid to look after.

Muffin sat in the box but refused to do anything.

"What's going on?" Michael said, coming up behind Maddy.

"I'm waiting for her to go potty. She's not going to get a T-R-E-A-T until she does."

"Why are you spelling that word?"

"If she hears it, she'll get excited and won't use the litter box." Maddy realized Rambo was jumping on her. "Would you please get him a D-O-G-G-I-E B-I-S-C-U-I-T while I wait for Muffin to go? They're in the red G-O-O-D-Y B-A-G on the counter. Watch your thumb."

Michael nodded. "Yeah, thanks." He found the bag and reached inside. Not only was there an assortment of treats, he found doggie bones of all shapes, sizes, and flavors. There were also more toys than most children had. Poor Maddy. She was obviously transferring all the love she would bestow on a baby to these hot dogs from hell. He offered the larger dachshund a biscuit, but the animal refused to come close to him.

"Hey, it's no skin off my teeth, buddy. Take it or leave it." He groaned inwardly. He'd been reduced to conversing with a dog. And not just any dog, mind you, this particular mutt appeared to be a dimwit. Finally, he set the dog biscuit on the counter, and the dog slunked to the floor with a defeated look. Michael cursed under his breath for loving a woman with such a dog, and tossed the biscuit to the floor. Rambo pounced on it.

"Any luck in there?" he asked Maddy.

"She's being stubborn as usual. That's okay, Muffin, I've got all day. You can sit there and pout till the cows come home, but you're not leaving that box until you do your business."

The thought that Maddy might stand in there all day made Michael anxious. How was he supposed to win his wife over if she was determined to stand over a dog until the animal finally decided to go to the bathroom?

This was going to be harder than he thought. He waited, but when there was no activity in the other room, Michael pulled on the larger pair of wading boots, grabbed his coat and gloves, and hurried outside.

Although the snow was still coming down, it had slowed considerably. He found a stick nearby and stuck it into the white mass, then pulled it up. He let off a big shiver. There was at least sixteen to eighteen inches on the ground, and heavy cloud cover hinted at more. Stepping very carefully, he walked to the edge of the cabin, then, moving cautiously, he turned down the side, heading in the direction of the woodshed. His boot struck something in the snow, and he used his hands to dig. He grinned when he found what he was looking for.

Inside the cabin, Michael shrugged off his coat and kicked off the boots. He glanced into the utility room to see if any progress had been made. Maddy was now sitting cross-legged beside the litter box, arms folded at her chest, clearly in a test of wills with the dachshund. He shook his head and went to the sink, where he turned on the faucet. The pipes below shook and clanged, and he prayed he'd wrapped them adequately. They faucet burped and sputtered, sending forth a rusty stream. He continued to let the water run until it was clear and sparkling. He grabbed the percolator, filled it with fresh water and coffee grounds, and plugged it in. Noting the pot on the stove was beginning to boil, he reached for the knob and turned it off.

Maddy shrieked with delight and began praising Muffin, leading Michael to believe the dog had not only tinkled but laid the golden egg as well. The animal followed her mistress to the kitchen, where she sat on her hind legs in anticipation of a treat. Maddy gave her a dog biscuit, while Rambo, possibly trying to pretend he'd never received his, tried to sit as prettily as his sister. He kept falling down, his paws sliding outward on the vinyl floor, so that he landed on his chest each time. Maddy finally offered them both a slice of ham while Michael looked on in disapproval.

"They have to eat something," she said defensively, "until I can get to their food." She saw the stream of water running from the spigot. A smile lit up her face. "You found the valve."

"Purely by accident," he said. "I was on my way out to the shed to see how much wood we had, and I almost tripped over the damn thing."

"Oh, and you're making coffee," she noted, hearing the percolator belch. "Thank you. I was dreading drinking instant."

With the coffee made, they each carried their cups to the living room. Maddy sat on the sofa. Michael took the chair. The dogs stayed behind, staring at the refrigerator as if they expected it to swing open and dole out more meat. After a few minutes Rambo jumped up, placed his paws on the door, and barked as though he could will it open. Once again, Muffin raised up on her hind legs and begged.

"You probably noticed a red Jeep stranded down the road," Maddy went on. "It belongs to me. In case you don't remember," she added.

Michael didn't answer right away. He didn't know if he should remember the Jeep or not, since he'd seen it right before he'd been knocked unconscious. He wished he knew more about amnesia; he couldn't afford to screw up. "Is there anything in it you need?" he finally asked, avoiding the question.

"Just food, clothes, firewood, and dog food."

"I'm sure we can think of a way to get it here."

"What we need is a big sled."

Michael nodded and sipped his coffee in silence. This would give him the opportunity to prove himself in an emergency. Maddy would discover she had nothing to fear as long as he was there to take care of her. A woman could talk about being strong and independent all she liked, but when it came to survival, she needed a man. Already, he could feel an idea forming in his mind. The shed! He could tear the boards down and build the sled from those. Might take a while, might even take a couple of days, since there would probably be a number of rotted boards to contend with.

"Do we have any rope?" Michael asked, already excited over his plan. He envisioned what the sled would look like and how it would glide through the snow when he pulled it. He only hoped the boards didn't crack the minute he stacked groceries or firewood on it.

"There's some yellow nylon rope in the utility room," Maddy told him. She smiled suddenly. "I'll bet *I* know what you're going to do. You're going to take down one of the doors and nail that nylon rope to it so you can pull it across the snow. Am I right?"

One of the doors? Michael stared back at her.

Maddy pointed to the door that opened into the utility room. "I knew that's what you'd come up with, since you once remarked how solid they are, unlike most doors, which are hollow inside. Of course, you probably don't remember that, nor would you remember those old snow skis you absolutely refused to throw away. Your tools are still here, even that rusty saw that you swore would come in handy one day. Guess that day has arrived, huh?"

Michael didn't know what to say. The fact that she'd come up with a brilliant solution to their problems, while he was still working on some half-baked scheme to tear down a storage shed, did little for his male ego. Her dogs came into the room, and Rambo automatically growled at the sight of Michael.

"What'd I do?" he asked Maddy, holding his hands out as if surrendering.

She waved it off. "It's just a guy thing. He's already determined this is his territory, and now it's a power struggle."

"Does this mean I'm going to have to sleep in my car tonight?"

She tried to look serious. "No, it just means the two

of you should spend some time together. So you can bond."

"Bond?"

Danny staggered down the hall, hair disheveled, mouth wide open in a yawn. "I'm starving. What's for breakfast?" he asked.

Maddy smiled. "I don't know. What do you feel like making us?"

The boy frowned. "Cooking is women's work."

"Wrong," Michael said. "Cooking is for the person who's hungriest."

Maddy looked surprised. She could count on one hand how many times Michael had cooked a meal in the five years they'd lived together, and those he'd cooked had been along the lines of grilled-cheese sandwiches and scrambled eggs. His mother, who'd given birth to five boys, each about a year apart, claimed she hadn't had time to train them to do things for themselves, she simply did it for them. Maddy discovered almost immediately after their marriage that Michael was helpless when it came to taking care of a household. Not that she had any room to judge. Having been raised by nannies and servants, she had been forced to learn to do even the simplest things for herself once she'd moved out on her own.

She wondered if Michael had found himself in the same predicament after their split.

"I don't know how to cook," Danny confessed meekly.

Maddy couldn't help but feel sorry for the boy. "Tell you what. Why don't you help Uncle Michael, and I'll make a nice breakfast. Just give me a second to change clothes." That brought a smile to his face.

"Let me get my toolbox," Michael said, stepping inside the utility room and reaching for it on a shelf. He found his saw hanging nearby. He grabbed it and turned around, almost bumping into Maddy. She looked curious. He realized he'd made another blunder.

"How'd you know where to find your tools?" she asked.

"Where else would they be? They'd rust in the shed."

"How'd you know about the shed?"

"Huh? Oh, I must've seen it last night when I pulled in."

"It's not visible from the front."

"And you mentioned last night how it collapsed and got the wood wet. Why are you asking me these questions?"

"Sorry. I was hoping you'd remembered something. Well, let me know if you need anything."

Michael sighed his relief as she made her way to the bedroom, dogs in tow. He didn't have to be a genius to know the only reason she was so worried about him was because she felt guilty for causing his injury. And he was a skunk for allowing her to continue to feel that way after the hurt his thoughtlessness had caused her. But how else was he supposed to prove how much he'd changed?

By the time he had the door off its hinge and Maddy announced breakfast, Michael had convinced himself he was doing the right thing. After all, he was trying to save their marriage, and with their divorce date fast approaching, he didn't have much time.

He washed his hands and sat down at the small table, a plate of fried eggs, bacon, and buttered toast in front of him. Muffin came up beside him and sat on her hind legs while Rambo followed Maddy about. She set two small bowls of cereal on the floor, and the dogs raced to them. Michael remained quiet, knowing they didn't have anything else to eat at the moment. Besides, a little cereal couldn't hurt. He picked up his fork.

"That's Danny's plate," Maddy said, picking it up and setting another one before him.

Michael glanced at his plate. "What's this?"

"Don't you recognize whole wheat toast and melon?"

The thought of eating dry toast was like eating a T-bone steak with only the bone, like having sex without the climax. "Am I allowed to have anything on my toast?"

She opened the refrigerator. "A little jam wouldn't hurt," she said, "although I wish you'd bought low-sugar. Luckily you brought plenty of oranges, so that should stop your hunger pains."

"Yes, I have every confidence it will," he said dully. Danny snickered. Michael shot him a dark look, but he was more interested in what was on the kid's plate. "Why can't I have bacon?" he asked.

"Sodium." Maddy made it sound like one of those dreaded new diseases for which there was no cure. "If you hope to lower your blood pressure, you're going to have to give up salt." She set her own plate down and joined them. "Not to mention the cigarettes," she added wryly.

"Cigarettes?" he said innocently.

"Danny said you were putting out more smoke than a neighborhood barbecue on your drive up last night."

Michael slid a glance in his nephew's direction, but the boy refused to meet his gaze. He glanced at Maddy's plate and saw the usual hard-boiled egg, toast, and orange slices. He'd always considered it a boring breakfast for somebody who didn't need to count calories or fat grams, but she preferred to eat light while getting in the extra protein she needed for the demands her job placed on her body.

"Do you think I'm overweight?" he asked, hoping to get Maddy's mind off his smoking. At the same time he wanted to see if she still found him attractive.

"It's really hard to tell with you sitting."

He slid from his chair. "How's this?"

"Turn around," she said.

He sucked his stomach in and tried to make himself taller.

Danny, in the process of drinking his milk, suddenly laughed so hard, he spewed it all over himself. "He's holding in his stomach, Aunt Maddy," the boy said, milk dripping from his nose. He grabbed his napkin and held it in place as he tried to get control of himself.

Maddy, who was doing her level best to keep a straight face, took one look at Danny and burst into hearty laughter. Tears streamed from their eyes.

Michael frowned and sat down. "I'm so glad the two of you find me entertaining," he muttered, and bit into his dry toast.

"I'm so sorry," Maddy said, trying hard to contain herself. She finally looked as though she might succeed, when Danny suddenly hiccuped, and they both collapsed into fresh peels of laughter.

"How about I slam that poker over my head again," Michael suggested. "That ought to be good for a few chuckles. Or I could try to get Rambo to bite my other thumb."

Maddy had to leave the room because she couldn't catch her breath. She moved to the living room and sat on the floor in front of the fireplace so she couldn't see Danny, who in turn hurried down the hall to the bedroom and closed the door. A grumbling Michael ate his breakfast and Maddy's, then sneaked a strip of bacon from a small plate on the stove. Every once in a while he'd hear Maddy chuckle from in front of the fireplace.

"Damn, Maddy, why don't you just go ahead and call me a big fat slob and be done with it."

She collapsed on the floor and covered her face with a throw pillow to muffle her laughter.

It was a good fifteen minutes before Maddy and Danny managed to quiet their giggles once and for all. Michael had cleared the table and filled a sink with hot sudsy water by the time she returned, looking for her plate.

"I hope you don't mind that I fed your breakfast to the kiddies," he lied, pointing to her pets, who watched from the hallway. "I figured it was the least I could do."

Maddy could see that he wasn't happy with her. His feelings were obviously hurt. "Michael, I wasn't laughing at you. I got tickled over Danny's antics."

"Just forget it."

"And no, I don't think you're overweight, but it's not important what I think. I'm not your doctor. I'm sure if he's seen some weight gain on you, he's concerned, since your father's been battling weight *and* high blood pressure for years now."

"Aunt Maddy knows what she's talking about," Danny piped in. "She teaches exercise classes, in case you don't remember."

"I'm a fitness trainer," Maddy corrected him, as she did anyone who referred to her as an exercise teacher. She'd spent a number of years studying to obtain her knowledge and skills, and she wanted people to know she was serious about her vocation. "I work in a gym, and I also have a private practice."

Michael suddenly had a great idea, one that might even win him time with Maddy after they returned home. "I'd like to hire you," he said after a moment. "I'm going to need all the help I can get."

She was more than a little surprised by the suggestion, and it showed. "I'm not taking new clients at the moment," she said. "I was only trying to help as a courtesy."

Not taking on new clients, he thought. That was rich. If she came to him with legal problems, he'd be only too happy to oblige, and he wouldn't think of charging her. "How am I supposed to know what to eat if you don't tell me?" he insisted. "What's to keep my blood pressure from shooting up again when I get home?"

"I probably have a copy of something in my car that'll help you. My personal physician keeps me up-to-date on nutritional plans for diabetes, heart disease, high

blood pressure, even various forms of cancer. I'll be glad
to discuss your diet with you."

"But you won't take me on as a client."

"That's correct."

"Even if it means the difference between life and
death?"

"I'll be happy to refer you to another fitness trainer
who has more experience than I do."

"That's not very professional of you, Maddy. You're
letting personal feelings get in the way."

"Once you've regained your memory, you'll understand why I feel the way I do."

Michael wished he didn't have to worry about it at
all. He remembered a time in high school he could wolf
down several fried eggs and a half pound of bacon with a
tall stack of toast slathered in real butter and not gain an
ounce. In college and law school he'd lived off junk and
fast food; he'd barely had time to toss something into
his mouth much less cook, in between work and school
and all the studying he'd had to do. He remembered the
healthy, wholesome dinners Maddy had cooked when
they'd lived together. She knew how to prepare food so
that he could eat a low-fat diet and not feel he was
missing anything. He'd been in pretty good shape too.

Of course, there were other perks to living with her.
Like climbing into bed at night and finding her next to
him, smelling like something out of this world. Maddy
was all woman, and she knew how to take care of herself. She had every kind of bath oil and specialty soap
you could think of—lavender, magnolia blossom, garde-
nia—and a dozen different sponges and gizmos for
washing that he could never remember what they were

called. And there were sweet-smelling candles and pot-
pourri in every room, sachets in her drawers and closet
that gave off a pleasant scent. The condo had smelled
like a flower garden when she'd lived there; now you
walked in the front door and thought you were in a beer
joint or pizza parlor.

He used to love to watch her fuss with herself, primp
before a mirror, paint her toenails, pluck her eyebrows,
and rub lotion all over. Everything about her fascinated
him; she was so perfect in every way. Making love to her
was a wonderfully sensuous experience. He knew he
would never tire of her.

But there were only so many hours in a day, and
after years of spending most of them working, he'd
gradually had less and less energy for his wife. He
dragged in late each night, ate a few bites, and went to
bed. Their lovemaking became infrequent, and they'd
had little time for conversation. He remembered looking at her from across the breakfast table one morning
and feeling very sad because they had drifted apart.

The worst part was not knowing what to do about it,
the hurt and disappointment he saw in her eyes every
time he looked at her. When he was home, he worried
about his cases at the office; at work he worried about
his marriage. She began locking the bathroom door
when she bathed, and he stopped reaching for her as
often in the night. Sometimes, after they made love and
he'd turned over to go to sleep, he thought he heard her
crying.

Then she'd become pregnant, and all communica-
tion had shut down. He'd accused her of doing it on
purpose, of trying to punish him for the long hours he

worked. Hadn't he made it perfectly clear from the beginning that he didn't want children? Didn't they have enough stress in their lives without adding to it?

He knew how destructive children were, how they wreaked havoc on a marriage. He'd watched his own poor parents deal with five boys. If the carpet and furniture weren't proof enough, all he had to do was look at his mother's weary face and the perpetual scowl on his father's. Michael could not remember a single time that his parents had gone to dinner or to a movie together when he was growing up.

He had not wanted those hardships in his own marriage. The luxury condominium Maddy's parents had purchased for them was strictly for adults and maybe a small pet here and there. He knew Maddy longed for a place in the country where she could have cats and dogs and horses, with enough land to plant a flower and vegetable garden. Which brought him to the next thing they didn't need: yard work. Neither of them had time for that sort of thing. They should be enjoying life in what little spare time they had.

He'd been blind and selfish. He'd assumed Maddy would automatically want what he wanted. As if she didn't have a mind of her own. Of course, he would agree to any of it if that's what it took to get her back. Even the part about having children. He was just that desperate.

"Michael, is something wrong?" Maddy asked, wondering why he was so quiet. "Does your head hurt?"

He looked up, saw the concern in her eyes. Once again, he knew it was based on guilt, but he was thankful to have even that from her. "I'm okay," he said. "I need to get back to work on that door while the snow has slackened off."

Maddy looked out the kitchen window and saw that he was right. "I'll help," she said. "With the three of us working, it shouldn't take long."

"Danny and I can handle it," he said.

"Yeah, us guys can handle it," Danny told her.

Maddy saw the proud look on her nephew's face and decided to go along with it. "I'll keep the home fires burning and the coffee and hot chocolate coming so you men can warm up in between runs. How's that?"

"Besides, Danny and I need to have one of those man-to-man talks, right?" He slapped the boy on his back.

The grin seemed to slide right off Danny's face. "*She* told you, didn't she?"

"*She* has a name, and I expect you to use it," Michael replied. "And it doesn't matter who told me. What you did was childish and irresponsible, not to mention inconsiderate as hell. What a perfect way to wish your folks Happy Thanksgiving."

Danny's face blazed with color. "You'd better be glad I came along," he said. "If it weren't for me, you'd have frozen to death in that snow. I can't believe you're sucking up to somebody who'd just as soon kill you as look at you." He turned for the hall.

Michael grabbed Danny's arm and held him in place. The boy's eyes popped wide in surprise. "Let's get something straight, pal," he said, between clenched teeth. "I don't know how you talk to your folks, but you will *not* use that tone here. Unless you want to spend the day with your nose in a corner."

Maddy felt like cheering but decided to stay out of it.

"You're not my father, you can't tell me what to do!" Danny shouted.

Michael pulled him closer. "Wanna bet?" The boy didn't answer. "And if you raise your voice to me again, I'll put you over my knee."

"Stop treating me like a baby," Danny said.

"You want to be treated like a man, *act* like one."

"You don't have any right to get on my case when you've screwed up your own life," the boy sputtered. "Everybody knows how crummy you were to Aunt Maddy. It's your fault she lost the baby. The only person you ever think about is yourself."

"That's enough, Danny," Maddy said.

"Your own family thinks she's better off without you."

Michael released him. He suddenly felt as if he'd been kicked in the gut. He wasn't aware his family knew about the miscarriage, but if they did, he certainly couldn't blame them for thinking the worst of him. He felt the same way. He stepped away from Danny. "You're right, kid," he said. "Who am I to give advice when I've done such a rotten job handling my own affairs?" He walked down the short hall to the bedroom and closed the door.

# SIX

Maddy felt sick at heart over the argument that had just taken place. She looked at her nephew. "What's gotten into you?" she demanded. "Who do you think you are, talking to your uncle that way?"

Danny tossed her an angry look. He didn't resemble the kid who'd been laughing uncontrollably only minutes before. "I can't believe you're taking up for him after what he did to you?"

"How do you know about my miscarriage? Your mother was the only one I told." She had called Brenda from the hospital after she'd lost the baby because there was nobody else to talk to, and because she knew her sister-in-law would cut her tongue out before repeating it. Nobody else in the family had even known she was pregnant.

"I heard my mom talking to you on the phone the day it happened," Danny said.

"You were eavesdropping?"

"I was coming into the kitchen for a snack, and I

heard her crying, so I backed out. The only reason I listened was 'cause I thought something had happened to Grandma or Grandpa."

"Your mother wouldn't have told the rest of the family," Maddy said knowingly. "That means *you* said something." Danny averted his gaze. "Well?" she insisted.

"Nobody else knows," he confessed. "I just said that."

"To be cruel?"

"He ticked me off."

"Remind me never to *tick* you off. You go straight for the jugular." She grabbed the broom and started sweeping the kitchen, hoping to work off some of her own anger and frustration. She looked up a moment later and found Danny still standing there.

"Do you need me to do something?" he asked.

She paused and leaned on the broom. She'd heard teenagers had mood swings, thanks to hormonal changes, but this kid was something else. The fact that he looked ashamed of himself, though, was a good sign. "Yes, as a matter of fact, there is something you can do for me. You can change your poor attitude. There's no way to know how long we'll be up here, and I'll not have you making trouble. As for my relationship with your uncle, that's absolutely none of your business."

He opened his mouth to say something, then seemed to think better of it.

Maddy went back to sweeping. "You know, Danny, you're going to have to learn how to get along with other people in this world if you plan to go out on your own." She heard the bedroom door open. Michael came down the hall and stepped into the utility room. Without a word, he went to work on the door.

The dogs kept their places behind the chair in the living room.

Danny watched his uncle for a few minutes. "Do you need some help?" he finally asked.

Michael didn't look his way. "No, I got it."

The boy went into the living room and plopped down on the sofa. Maddy suspected he was bored. She decided to leave him be. He had chosen to run away, and he would have to deal with the consequences. She finished sweeping the floor, then wiped down the cabinets, all the appliances, and mopped the floor. The place wasn't in bad shape. The realtor who had the listing lived in the foothills and checked the cabin from time to time. She had even found someone to clean it every other month so she herself wouldn't have to make the long drive.

Maddy had decided it was well worth paying someone to look after it so she didn't have to deal with all the memories. She and Michael had been sitting on that very sofa when she'd broken the news of her pregnancy. She'd expected him to be shocked. Shock didn't come close to describing his reaction. He'd even accused her of doing it on purpose.

The fetus had died in its tenth week. Maddy had awakened that morning with a backache and abdominal pain. She'd started bleeding soon after Michael left for work. Her doctor had confirmed her suspicions shortly afterward when he examined her, and she'd been sent on to the hospital. She was certain it was her fault, that all her exercising had caused the miscarriage, but a kind older nurse explained that just wasn't the case.

She had to look toward the future now. She'd been told she could get pregnant again, but that was not a risk she was willing to take. She supposed it had something to do with losing a baby and walking out on a husband, all in two days, but it had taught her she never wanted to open herself up to that kind of pain again. If she was acting like a coward, so be it.

She only wished she wasn't still so attracted to Michael. Before his career had taken over their lives, they had been as close as two people could be. Their love-making had been the stuff of poetry and love songs, painstakingly gentle one moment, then fierce and all-consuming the next.

Maddy felt giddy and dreamy-eyed just thinking about it.

Michael paused in his work and looked up. "Is something wrong?"

"Huh?" Maddy blushed. Lord, he'd caught her staring. What was wrong with her? "I was just, uh, wondering if you should be doing all that work. What if it makes your condition worse?" Okay, so it was a feeble excuse, but it was the only thing that came to mind.

"I'm okay," he assured her, but something in her look convinced him there was more going on than just her concern for his safety. He planned to find out what it was. He smiled the smile that she'd once confided made her knees quake. It would never occur to her that he was doing it on purpose, what with him not remembering. "I could go for another cup of coffee."

"Coming right up." Maddy grabbed clean cups from

the cabinet. Her hands trembled so badly, one would have thought she'd been struck with palsy. "Danny, would you like some hot chocolate?" she asked. He muttered something that sounded like no. Maddy shrugged and filled two mugs and placed them on the table. She reached for her chair to pull it out, but Michael was quicker.

"Thank you," she said, remembering how impressed she'd been with his manners the first time they'd gone out. She learned later that Brenda was responsible for teaching all the Kelly brothers how to behave with a young lady. She sat down and waited for Michael to join her.

He took the chair opposite her and sipped his coffee. "Well, I know we didn't split up over your coffee," he said. "This is the best I've ever tasted."

"I always put a pinch of salt in it."

"A trick your mother taught you, no doubt," he said, although he knew that wasn't the case.

Maddy smiled. "You *have* forgotten a lot. I doubt my mother has ever made a pot of coffee in her life. Actually, I learned it from our butler, Mr. Yates."

Michael had met Yates. A gentleman if ever there was. The man adored Maddy and she him. "Ah, the butler. Every home should have at least one."

"He was like a father to me. I was close to all the staff, actually."

Michael nodded as though hearing it for the first time. He knew why Maddy was so devoted to the servants. Her parents had had little time for her, what with their busy social calendar. Fortunately, their employees had adored her and had seen to it that she was well cared for.

"Yates died five months ago," Maddy said sadly.

Michael snapped to attention. Yates dead? He didn't want to believe it, didn't want to think of Maddy having to mourn his passing all alone. "I'm sorry," he said, and meant it. "How did he die?"

"Heart attack." Maddy looked sad. "I didn't even know he had a bad heart. Nobody knew. But that's the way Yates was. He kept things like that to himself." She took another sip of coffee, promising herself she wouldn't get teary-eyed. "He was from Vermont. The service was beautiful. I was the only one in my family to show. My parents couldn't change their plans to attend the funeral of a man who'd run their home for thirty years. However," she continued, her lips twisted into a cynical smile, "they had hundreds of orchids flown in. That was Mr. Yates's favorite flower."

Michael knew her parents had a flair for the theatrical; his and Maddy's wedding on Martha's Vineyard had resembled something out of a fairy tale. Her parents had ferried in coaches and white horses and a dozen white stretch limousines for attending dignitaries. They hired three catering services and a French chef from a four-star restaurant. They even rented an entire hotel and several houses on the Vineyard to accommodate the wedding guests, as well as a fleet of golf carts to get them around the island. The prewedding parties had lasted for three days, and he felt bad for his family, who looked out of place next to senators and congressmen and various celebrities. By the time he and Maddy left for a two-week honeymoon in Hawaii, she'd been near tears. She had asked for a simple wedding.

They had returned to a mountain of wedding gifts—a dozen toaster ovens, two dozen coffeemakers, way too many mixers and blenders and cookware, and enough crystal and silver and fine china to fill the dining room of a fancy hotel. Maddy had donated much of it to women's shelters and other nonprofit organizations. And even though they'd moved into a three-hundred-and-fifty-thousand-dollar condominium with Italian-marble columns and flooring, a gourmet kitchen, and a massive Jacuzzi in every bathroom, Maddy hadn't liked it. Which was why she'd had no qualms about moving out and leaving it for him to sell.

Michael noted the deep sadness in Maddy's eyes and wished he could say or do something to make her feel better, wished he'd been there to comfort her when she'd first learned about Yates's death. He hated the thought of her suffering alone. But then, she'd always been alone, even more so while she was married to him. He probably wouldn't have been able to attend the funeral with her either, nice guy that he was.

"I'm sorry for your loss," he finally said, "and I'm sorry you had to go through it by yourself."

"Thank you," she said. "The one thing that gives me comfort is knowing I'll see him again one day."

Michael drained the rest of his coffee. "Well, I've been putting it off as long as I can," he said. "Better get back to work."

Maddy rinsed their cups. Danny was still sitting on the sofa, staring straight ahead. She wondered if he was beginning to regret leaving home, and she hoped that was the case. Maybe she could help out in that department.

Grabbing her cleaning supplies from beneath the sink, she searched for a can of furniture polish and an old rag, and carried them into the living room. "Danny, I need you to help me out with a few chores," she said, and thought his eyeballs would pop right out of his head. "Would you please dust and vacuum for me while I scrub the bathroom?"

"But that's women's work."

"It is?" she said innocently. "Where does it say that?"

"My dad doesn't do that kind of stuff."

"Honey, your father sometimes works two jobs so that your mom can stay home with you kids. I think that pretty much excuses him from domestic chores." She handed him the polish and dust cloth and left the room. As she started down the hall with her cleaning supplies, she peeked inside the utility room and found Michael hard at work, sawing the tips off a pair of child's skis. She cleaned the bathroom thoroughly, smiling to herself when she heard Danny running the vacuum cleaner. In the bedroom, she put fresh sheets on the bed and dusted. By the time she finished, she found Michael, in jacket, gloves, and wading boots, lugging the makeshift sled through the front door.

"Wait," she said. "I have to give you my keys." She reached for her purse.

"You locked your Jeep?" he ask, amused.

She handed him her key ring. "I always lock it. Why?"

"No reason." He tucked them into his pocket and started off.

"Michael?"

He paused and looked over his shoulder. "Yeah?"

"Please be careful."

"Don't tell me you're worried about me."

She blushed. "You have a serious head injury. Why wouldn't I be worried?"

It wasn't the answer he'd been hoping for. "I'll be fine," he mumbled. "Close the door before you catch a cold." He turned and gave his sled a hard tug.

Maddy closed the door and hurried into the living room so she could watch Michael from a window. Danny, having completed his chores, looked on miserably.

"Would you look at that?" she said. "A few more inches and the snow would be up to his knees. He can barely walk through all of it."

"At least it isn't snowing as hard as it was," Danny said. "I still don't know how he plans to pull that sled all by himself."

"I hope he doesn't step in a hole," Maddy fretted. She turned anxious eyes to Danny. "Lord, what if he did step in a hole and ended up spraining his ankle, or worse, breaking it? What would we do then?"

Maddy hurried toward the door and grabbed the wading boots and her coat.

"What are you doing?" Danny said. "Uncle Michael told you to stay inside."

"I can't let him exert himself like that," she said frantically. "He's got a head injury, for Pete's sake.

What if he suddenly forgets what he's doing out there? What if he just wanders off and freezes to death?"

"I'll go," Danny said, taking the boots from her.

"You!"

He looked offended. "I happen to be a lot stronger than I look."

"That's not what I meant. Michael already said he didn't need your help."

"So maybe I'll apologize." He pulled on the boots and reached for his coat while Maddy grabbed a knitted cap and gloves.

"I don't know if this is a good idea, Danny," she said. "Your mother will kill me if something happens to you."

"Please don't treat me like a baby, Aunt Maddy. I'm so sick of it."

"Okay, okay." She handed him everything he would need. Once he was suitably dressed, she opened the door and held it for him. "Please be careful."

"I'll be fine," he said. "Now close the door before you catch cold."

Maddy did as he said and reclaimed her spot in front of the window.

Michael had never seen so much snow. Surely, the storm had set some kind of record. Luckily, the home-made sled seemed to be working well. He only wished it'd been his idea instead of Maddy's. It wouldn't be long before they cleared the snow, and he still hadn't thought of a way to impress her.

He had a disturbing thought. What if he never managed to impress her because she wasn't interested in him anymore and never would be? She had built a new life. What if it included a new man as well?

Michael felt his shoulders slump. He wasn't easily defeated, and he wasn't one to let others have power over his emotions, but damned if Maddy didn't have him running scared.

He had to win her back. That was his top priority. Nothing else mattered.

He'd reached her Jeep. He turned the sled around so he wouldn't have to do it after it was loaded. The cold had already seeped through his gloves and cap, and he could feel the lump on the back of his head beginning to throb. There was no time to waste. He unlocked the door, wondering as he did so why Maddy had felt it necessary to take precautions against thieves, when the snow was so deep it could swallow a big dog.

Not that caution was a bad thing. The city of Charlotte had grown considerably over the past few years, and the crime rate had grown right along with it. On second thought, he was glad Maddy was using extra care these days.

He opened the door. Inside, were a number of grocery sacks, a large ice chest, Maddy's luggage, and a load of wood that he figured would see them through several days. He planned to move the wood from the shed inside the cabin first chance he got, but at least they wouldn't have to worry about running out anytime soon. He shivered and reminded himself to hurry. He reached for a bag, and as he turned he saw Danny walking toward him.

"What the hell are you doing out here? I thought I told you—"

"I know what you told me, Uncle Michael, but Aunt Maddy was driving me crazy. She's worried sick about you."

Michael perked up. "She is?"

Danny took the sack from him and set it on the sled. "Oh, you shoulda seen her carrying on back there. It's enough to make a man want to run screaming into a blizzard and get lost."

Michael chuckled. He no longer felt cold; in fact, he felt kind of warm and fuzzy all over. "She's really worried, huh?"

Danny shook his head sadly. "You got it bad, don'cha?"

"Is it that noticeable?"

"Yeah. I don't think I'd let her see that look just yet, on account of her divorcing you and all."

Michael reached for another sack and handed it to the boy. He was glad to have someone to confide in. "I've got to change her mind about that, Danny."

"You planning to try and win her back?"

"I don't know if she'll have me. She's gone to a lot of trouble to avoid me since our separation—getting a new job, moving to an undisclosed location." He saw Danny's grin and knew he'd made a mistake. "Damn."

"So you never really lost your memory after all," the boy said. "Don't worry, I won't say anything."

"Actually, I did lose my memory for several hours." He moved to the back of the Jeep and opened the door so he could slide out the cooler. It took some work, but he managed to get it to the sled. "We'll have to come back for the rest," he said, once he'd put Maddy's luggage on board. He closed the doors to the Jeep and hurried to the front of the sled with the nylon rope snaked across the snow. They each grabbed hold of it and tugged.

"I don't understand something," Danny said, grunting as he tried to pull his share of the load. "Why are you pretending you have amnesia?"

"It's simple. She can't hate me while I'm hurt and don't remember what I did wrong. The minute she finds out it's really me in residence, she's liable to clobber me over the head again. I have to try to convince her I'm a different man from the one she walked out on. And I *am* different, Danny. There's nothing I wouldn't do for that woman."

They moved slowly due to the depth of the snow. "Look, I'm really, really, sorry for what I said earlier, Uncle Michael. Most of what I said was a lie anyway. My mom is the only one in the family that knows about the baby. I just happened to overhear the conversation she had with Aunt Maddy the day it happened. From now on I'm just going to keep my mouth shut. All it does is get me into trouble."

"Just try to start thinking before you speak," Michael told him. "You can never take back the hurtful things you say to people. Believe me, I know."

Danny glanced around at the scenery. "You know, if I had this place I'd stay here all the time."

"What would you do for work?"

"I wouldn't have to work 'cause I'd hunt for my food. I'd be, uh . . ."

"Self-sufficient?" Michael offered.

"Yeah, that. Then I won't have to put up with my mean old man anymore."

"You know, Danny, I have a friend who handles child-abuse-and-neglect cases. I could talk to him on your behalf."

Danny's face turned a bright red. "I don't think—"

"I know your dad has a temper, son. Does he knock you around?"

"No, but he took my stereo away, and he makes me spend two hours a day in my room doing my homework."

"Did he bar the doors and windows? I've heard of parents doing that to their kids. I've heard stories that would make you sick to your stomach. Damn, it's cold out here. Anyway, if your parents are mistreating you, odds are they're mistreating your little sisters as well. It's up to you to step forward. I can have the three of you removed so fast, they won't know what hit them."

"No!" Danny faced him, green eyes flashing angrily. "I can't believe you'd actually do something like that to them when you know how much they love us. Why, Aunt Maddy even said my dad works two jobs just so my mom can stay home with us."

"So, you're saying they're pretty good parents, after all?" Michael said, grinning.

The boy gave a grunt of disgust and tugged hard on the rope. "Ah, I should have known you were just messing with me. Ha, ha, very funny."

"If you think that's funny, wait till you hear my turkey call." They slipped and stumbled through the rest of their journey, laughing hard as they tried to outdo the other with turkey sounds.

Maddy had the fire blazing and fresh coffee waiting by the time Michael and Danny brought in their first load. She also had water bubbling on the stove for hot chocolate. She immediately filled two cups and unloaded the groceries while the two men sipped their drinks.

Checking the cooler, Maddy found the meat and refrigerated items icy cold to the touch, but not frozen. She pulled the turkey out and slit open the plastic covering so she could wash the bird. It wasn't huge, but it was a respectable size and would provide leftovers for a couple of days. Since it was close to lunchtime, she decided she would serve Thanksgiving dinner that evening. The bags she used to bake her turkeys in usually cut the cooking time in half.

Michael gazed at his wife from over the rim of his coffee cup as she prepared the turkey. Had he known he would be spending the holiday with her, he wouldn't have dreaded it so much. She was the picture of domesticity, her shoulder-length hair pulled back, a clean apron tied around her waist. She had a tempting backside, made even more so by the tight jeans she wore, and the cropped, dusky pink sweatshirt that rose beguilingly when she moved, offering him a glimpse of honey-colored flesh that made him forget about everything else. She reached into an overhead cabinet, and the hem of her shirt inched up her spine. He would have given his entire retirement account to have her turn around slightly and flash that delectable navel. He sighed heavily.

"Are you hot yet?" Danny said.

"Huh?" Michael glanced at him quickly. Was he

that obvious? He could almost imagine his eyes rolling in his head and steam spewing out each ear.

"Have you warmed up enough to go back out?"

"Oh." Michael took a shaky breath. Warm didn't come close to describing how he was feeling, and if he stood up, it was likely his nephew would figure out his problem in one glance. "Let me finish my coffee," he said, although he was in no hurry to leave the warm kitchen and the woman who made it seem even more cozy.

"I'm going to visit the dogs for a minute," the boy said.

"They're in the bedroom," Maddy told him. "Be sure to keep the door closed."

Michael was only vaguely aware of Danny leaving the room; his eyes were trained on his wife. He didn't know what she was looking for, but as she searched through one cabinet after another, she left the doors standing open. How many times had he warned her against that very thing? And how many times had she knocked herself silly as a result?

"Uh, Maddy—" he began, then winced when her noggin collided with the corner of one cabinet door.

"Ouch!" Maddy cried.

Michael jumped up and hurried toward her, closing cabinet doors in his path. "I knew that was going to happen. Here, let me see how bad it is." He tilted her face back slightly. A red welt lay in her hairline. "It didn't break the skin, but there'll probably be a bruise." He held up three fingers. "How many do you see?"

"Eight. But I was never good at math. Do you think I'll need plastic surgery?"

"I'm afraid plastic surgery won't work in your case. You'll just have to be scarred for life. Probably, no man will ever look at you, so you might want to reconsider divorcing me."

"Oh, my. I think I may have amnesia."

It took only a second to realize she was kidding. "Oh, boy," he said, affecting a serious tone. "Do you know your name?"

She looked thoughtful. "No, but I think I come from royalty. I seem to recall being addressed as Queen something-or-other."

Grinning, Michael took one of her hands in his. "You're Queen Mary, named after a prestigious ship. And I'm your most trusted servant, here to please you in every way, if you get my drift." He gave her a hearty wink.

The touch of his hands on hers sent Maddy's stomach aflutter. She tried to hide her discomfort. "Does the king know about this?"

"The king is old and blind and deaf."

"The poor thing. I must go to him."

"He still manages to drink and gamble and run with tainted women, though, which is why you have no qualms about taking lovers."

"Oh, is that all." She tried to pull away.

"I've also seen him kick your dogs from time to time."

Her eyes narrowed dangerously. "I'll kill him."

The bedroom door opened, and her dachshunds darted out before Danny could grab them. "Who's that?" Maddy whispered, nodding toward the boy.

"He empties the palace chamber pots," Michael replied, a split second before Rambo sank his teeth into the hem of his jeans and tugged with all his might. Michael sighed and shook his head sadly.

"What's going on?" Danny asked, his eyes widening at the sight before him.

"Your Aunt Maddy hit her head on a cabinet door." He glanced once more at her wound. "You should be okay as long as you remember rule number one."

"Which is?"

"Don't leave dangerous, life-threatening cabinet doors open." He examined one carefully as if inspecting it for further hazards. "These things should come with warning labels." He turned to Danny. "Guess we'd better go get that wood." He crossed the room, dragging the dog along with him. "We'll have to hurry. Your aunt's not safe here, and I don't know how long this dog's going to last with me dragging him through the snow."

Maddy hurried over to Michael and pried the dog loose while Muffin sat up and begged for attention as well. Holding Rambo by the collar, she watched the two men bundle up and pull on the wading boots. She couldn't help thinking how much Michael resembled the man she'd fallen in love with more than six years earlier. Of course, that was before he'd become consumed with his job, before he'd forgotten how to laugh and have fun.

She prayed the roads would be cleared soon.

Before she fell in love with Michael all over again.

# SEVEN

Michael leaned back on the sofa, propped his feet on the coffee table, and gazed into the fire. He was one contented man. At least for now. Maddy's Thanksgiving dinner had hit the spot. She knew how to do things with food that were almost sinful, but it still came out healthy and wholesome. Who else could prepare a low-fat version of strawberry shortcake and have it taste so good? He was going to have to learn how she did it and get off his diet of junk food.

A lightbulb flashed in his head.

He could ask her to teach him how to cook!

Michael smiled at his own clever thinking. What better way to spend time with Maddy than standing shoulder to shoulder in the kitchen, dicing and slicing. If she truly had been as worried about him as Danny said, she would be only too happy to show him how to prepare healthy meals that would help in his battle to lower his blood pressure. Besides, Maddy loved to cook;

she'd even expressed a desire to write a cookbook, using recipes she'd experimented with over the years.

If only he could keep Danny occupied. The kid would create havoc in the kitchen and ruin any chances of Maddy and him rekindling their relationship. What worried him even more was the possibility of a plow coming through in the next day or two. Well, maybe not. He'd listened to the news on his car radio while Maddy was cooking dinner, and he'd learned the storm, which was the worst in ten years, had crippled a significant portion of the northwestern region of the state, both in the mountains and foothills. Hundreds of families were without power and stranded motorists littered the highways and back roads. He knew emergency workers would take care of those in life-threatening situations first.

Maddy swept into the room, bringing with her the scent of lilac from her bath. Her hair was still damp, but it had already begun to curl beguilingly around her face. She had traded in his pajama shirt for a pair of mint-green satin pajamas and matching robe. On her feet were furry white bunny slippers. One of the bunnies was missing a floppy ear, and Michael couldn't help but smile as he considered what might have happened to it.

The dachshunds suddenly appeared. Rambo paused and growled at Michael, but Maddy hushed him as she spread one of the blankets on the floor before the fire and sat down. Her pets situated themselves on either side of her.

"Don't tell me Danny's already asleep," Michael said.

"He's lying on the bed reading a detective magazine. I'm sure his mother will appreciate that."

"I suspect there are times his mother would let him play on a busy highway if it meant a little peace and quiet."

Maddy chuckled. "I read some of that magazine last night," she said, "and although the stories scared me half to death, there wasn't a lot of blood and gore in them. I say if it holds Danny's interest, let him read it. We can always worry about him becoming a sociopath once we return him to his parents."

"You'll be happy to know there are at least a half dozen more of those magazines in that cabinet over there. I found them way in the back when I was looking for extra space to stash some of the firewood."

"I guess the previous owners left them behind." She studied him as she spoke. She had never seem him look so relaxed, his hair slightly mussed, his clothes wrinkled. The Michael she knew was always impeccably dressed, clean-shaven, not a hair out of place. Even when he jogged he looked like he belonged in a Nike commercial. "You certainly look comfortable," she said.

"I *am* comfortable. Thanks to the wonderful meal you prepared. I was just thinking how I should get you to teach me how to cook. Good, healthy food," he added. "I've obviously been eating the wrong things, or my blood pressure wouldn't be so high."

Maddy was warmed by the compliment about her cooking, but she had no desire to give him lessons, any more than she wanted to help him with health and fitness. She knew the less time she spent with him the better. That was a tall order at the moment, considering they were cooped up in a three-room cabin. Once the roads were clear, she planned to be gone.

"I'll be glad to share some of my recipes with you," she said after a moment.

Michael was able to read between the lines. She didn't want to spend any more time with him than she had to. Not that he blamed her after the past they'd shared, but disappointment weighed heavily on him nevertheless. Didn't he deserve a second chance? He had to win her over, prove that he was a different man than the one she'd walked out on. And he *was* different in some ways. It had taken losing her to make him realize how much he loved her. He now knew she was the most important thing in the world to him.

As he gazed at her Michael couldn't believe the many evenings and weekends he'd spent at the office working instead of going home to her. Home where he'd belonged. So much time lost. There was no retrieving those missed days and nights, but he could make up for it if she gave him half a chance.

"You have to realize that your diet isn't the only thing pushing your blood pressure up," Maddy continued, drawing him from his thoughts. "It has a lot to do with your lifestyle. You're a typical type A personality, Michael. It won't be easy for you to change what's ingrained in you."

"Even if it means the difference between life and death?" he asked. "Or if it hampers my chances for a meaningful relationship? You underestimate me, Maddy. I may not be able to remember my past at the moment, but I damn sure know what's inside of me. There's not much I can't do once I put my mind to it." He stood and walked to the fire. After stirring it and adding another log, he looked out the front window. The snow wasn't coming down as hard.

"Michael?"

He turned, surprised to find Maddy standing directly behind him, only inches away. He hadn't even heard her get up. "What is it?"

"I have no right to suggest you're not capable of change. And it's not my place to point out what I feel are shortcomings in your personality."

"Oh, but it is," he said. "You obviously know me better than anyone else." It hurt him to look at her when all he wanted to do was touch her and kiss her until they were both dizzy. "I'm sorry if I let you down, Maddy," he said. Without thinking, he raised one hand to her cheek in a caress. "Try not to hate me too much, okay?"

His hand was rough against her cheek, and it made her feel protected, cherished. The feelings were as welcome as a cool rain on a hot summer day, and she found herself yearning for more. The thought jolted her. She had no business allowing it to go on, but as she raised her own hand to pull his away, their gazes locked and her fingers froze around his wrist.

What was she doing? she asked herself. Why was she standing there letting him look at her and touch her that way? Had she lost her poor mind? It had taken too many months of learning to live without Michael's touch. She wasn't about to fall into that old trap. Besides, she'd promised herself she'd never again rely on someone else for comfort. Strength came from within.

Yet she couldn't seem to find the energy to remove his hand from her cheek.

"I don't hate you, Michael," she said, trying to keep her voice under control, despite the fact she couldn't seem to catch her breath. Her heart was pounding so hard, she was certain he could hear the echo inside her rib cage. "I thought I did when we first split, but I was mostly angry at the time."

She didn't hate him. He supposed it was a start, Michael told himself, although he wished for more. How could she simply have stopped loving him after all they'd meant to each other?

Well, he hadn't stopped loving her and never would, for that matter. He wanted her just as much now as he had the first time he'd laid eyes on her. Even more. She might not love him anymore, but she didn't despise him either. That meant he had a fighting chance, and that was all he needed.

She was still grasping his wrist. That, too, had to mean something. Couldn't she feel his pulse beating erratically? Her touch thrilled him, especially after he'd lived without it all these months. She had beautiful hands, soft and gentle and loving. He remembered how they'd felt stroking his hair or toying with the curls on his chest. She had been many things to him—companion and confidante, lover and nurturer, helpmate and best friend. He had lost a lot when she'd walked out on him.

His gaze darkened as it held hers. Without breaking eye contact, he turned his hand and captured her own, then brought it to his lips. He pressed a kiss against her open palm. He could smell the soap she'd used to bathe herself, and the lotion she'd applied afterward. He groaned inwardly at the mental image he had of those same delicate hands closing around his sex, stroking him to hardness.

He could feel himself getting aroused, and he cursed his wayward body for reacting to the situation in such a way.

Maddy shivered as his warm mouth made contact with the very center of her palm, sending delightful tingles up her arm and causing an ache deep inside her. Emotion welled up at the back of her throat at the tender act. He was so stunningly virile, exuding masculinity from every pore, yet his touch was the gentlest thing she'd ever known.

She knew what those lips were capable of.

But it was sheer craziness to allow this to go on. She had absolutely no business letting Michael do what he was doing to her, even if it did feel wonderful. She had struggled long and hard to get him out from under her skin, and she wasn't about to go through all that again.

"Michael, please don't." She spoke in a broken whisper.

He didn't miss the pleading in her voice, or the glistening eyes that told him she was very near tears. The poor woman obviously couldn't bear his touch. He released her abruptly. A chill silence ensued. Without a word, he turned and strode to the door.

Anxiety spurted through Maddy when she saw him reach for his coat and gloves. "Where are you going?" she asked.

"I want to hear the latest weather report."

She crossed the room. His massive chest and shoulders filled the coat he wore. She could feel the power that coiled within him, could sense his restlessness. And his anger. "But it's so cold."

"Lucky for me my car has a heater." He reached for the door handle, then paused. "Besides, it'll do you good to have me out of your hair for a while. It must've been a rude shock to run into me way up here after all you did to get me out of your life." He let himself out before she could respond.

Michael stepped outside, cursing the bone-chilling wind that waited. The snow was deep; he staggered and stumbled like a Saturday-night drunk as he made his way to his car and climbed in. It offered about as much relief as a refrigerator on its lowest setting. He started the engine and waited.

He could feel himself scowling. He was ticked. Not to mention hurt and disappointed. Women thought they held the monopoly where emotions were concerned, but they were wrong. Just because guys didn't have periods or bear children didn't mean they didn't feel pain just as strongly as females. Men just went to a lot more trouble to hide it.

He knew what pain was. It was knowing that you'd blown the best thing that ever happened to you. It was knowing that you might never get it back again.

It was watching the woman you loved recoil at your touch.

Michael's mood was no better when he stepped inside the cabin a couple of hours later. He found it dark and cold, the fire having burned out, leaving a few red embers behind that barely gave off enough light for him to see. Heaving a weary sigh, he kicked off his shoes at the door and turned for the living room. He heard a low growl and braced himself as something darted from the shadows and flung itself at his foot, like a creature out of a Stephen King novel. It sank its fangs into the hem of his jeans.

"Hello, Rambo," he said. "Thanks for waiting up." Michael started for the fireplace, then cursed under his breath when the animal refused to let go. "Okay, pal," he mumbled, unfastening the metal button at his waist. "I don't feel like dragging a twenty-pound sausage around, so you can have the damn jeans if it'll make you happy." He shoved down the zipper and pulled them off. "Here, go for it," he said, tossing the pants aside. The dog pounced on them as if he'd just been handed a thick porterhouse steak.

Michael crossed the room in his Calvin Klein boxers and went about building a new fire, trying not to step on Danny, who was tucked inside a sleeping bag on the floor. He spied a black nose peeping out of the opening and realized Muffin was in the bag as well. Maddy had placed a couple of blankets on the sofa, but there was no way to open it into a bed with Danny camped out in front of it.

Once he had a fire going, Michael shrugged out of his coat and hung it near the door. He went into the kitchen and grabbed a diet drink from the refrigerator. He paused when he spied the bottle of white wine on the top shelf. He pulled it out and noticed about half of it was gone. Maddy must've had a couple of glasses after he'd left. She seldom drank anything other than juice or water. He was no sleuth, but he figured the missing wine accounted for the fact that the fire had been allowed to burn down.

He set the bottle back in the refrigerator and closed the door. He'd only taken two sips of his soft drink when he realized he was shivering. The kitchen was freezing; he suspected the bedroom would be much worse. He felt bad now for sitting in his car so long, but how was he to know Maddy would end up conking out without checking the fire? Besides, he'd had a lot of thinking to do, and he'd needed to be alone to do it.

Michael had come to terms with the fact that he was wasting his time where his wife was concerned, and the sooner he got them out of there the better. He would send off flares tomorrow and hope somebody saw them. It was only fair to Maddy that he get out of her life once and for all.

He'd been a fool to think she might still have feelings for him after the way he'd behaved, a bigger fool for pining away after her all these months when he should have been rebuilding his life. Once help arrived and he was certain she'd be okay, he would go home and pick up the pieces. It wouldn't be easy. It would be the hardest thing he'd ever had to do.

Michael glanced down the hall and wondered if Maddy was okay. Perhaps he should wake her and insist she move to the sofa until the heat spread to the rest of the cabin. He might have let her down as a husband, but he wasn't about to risk her health and welfare.

Rambo was still gnawing on his jeans as Michael turned on the hall light and made his way toward the bedroom. The door stood half-open. He peered in and called Maddy's name softly. He thought he heard a whimper.

"Maddy?" No answer. He stepped inside and hurried to the bed. "Maddy, honey, are you okay?"

She opened her eyes. "I'm cold," she said, her teeth chattering so badly, he could barely make out the words.

He sat on the bed and reached for her hand. It was icy cold. "The fire went out, babe. I just built another one. Why don't you come into the living room until it has time to warm up back here?"

"I'm too tired." She curled up tighter, as though she were trying to make herself into a ball. "And cold."

"Okay, sit tight for a minute," he said. "I'll be right back." He raced down the hall toward the living room. Rambo had dragged his jeans closer to the fire and was sleeping on them. He opened his eyes when Michael passed, yawned wide, and went back to sleep.

Michael grabbed the blankets from the sofa that Maddy had used to make his bed, and he took turns holding each one before the fire, warming them on both sides until they were toasty. He almost ran down the hall to the bedroom. He found Maddy dozing, but the frown on her face told him she wasn't comfortable.

Holding the blankets in one hand, he swept the covers from the bed. Maddy cried out in protest. He immediately covered her with the warm blankets, and her sighs of pleasure brought a smile to his face. He tucked the warm blankets around her, then piled the others on top, hoping to insulate the heat from the ones below.

"Thank you, Michael," she said in a dreamy, contented voice. "Where did you get these extra blankets?"

Now he was beginning to shiver. "They were on the sofa."

She opened her eyes. "But those were for you. You'll never be able to keep warm with just a sheet."

"I'll be okay, Maddy," he said, teeth chattering. "Just get some sleep."

"Listen to you, you're freezing to death. I'll never be able to sleep knowing I took your blankets." She sighed. "Get in the bed, Michael. Hurry, before you catch pneumonia."

He stared at her, slack-jawed, wondering if he'd heard right. "What did you say?"

She pulled the covers aside. "Get in. We'll have to sleep close so we can share our body heat." When he simply stood there, she gave an impatient huff. "Don't just stand there looking at me as though I've grown horns. We're talking survival here."

Michael nodded dumbly and climbed into bed, burrowing beneath the blankets. She turned her back to him and scooted close so they were lying spoon fashion. As he lay there, pressed against her softness, enveloped in her scent, only one coherent thought entered his mind.

*Eureka!*

# EIGHT

Michael discovered right away that it was not going to be easy to fall asleep. Maddy, on the other hand, had drifted off with no trouble. Which only proved her offer to share her bed had been of a humanitarian nature and not an invitation to love.

He gritted his teeth, wishing he could will a certain part of his anatomy to call it a night so he could finally get some rest. But taking into account how long it had been since he'd known the pleasures of a woman, specifically his wife, he could hardly blame his poor erection for doing what came naturally.

Maddy shifted in her sleep, and Michael groaned inwardly when her behind brushed against his swollen sex.

It was going to be a long night.

After what seemed an eternity, although in truth was only twenty minutes if the alarm clock was at all accurate, Michael slipped out of bed and made his way down the hall to the living room. Rambo had joined his sister in Danny's sleeping bag, dragging Michael's jeans in with him. One leg stuck out of the top of the bag as though protesting the overcrowding inside. Michael could only shake his head and wonder what went on in the minds of dachshunds.

He stirred the fire, added another log, and sat in the chair, shivering and wishing he had a blanket. It struck him as odd that he was waiting for the cabin and one part of his body to heat up while another part of his body was having a devil of a time cooling down. He regretted his decision to toss Rambo his jeans, but he suspected all hell would break loose if he tried to retrieve them. His other clothes were in a suitcase somewhere; the last time he'd seen it Maddy had been lugging it down the hall toward the bedroom to make room for the firewood in the living room. He'd probably wake up everybody, including the dogs, if he tried to find it.

He couldn't hold his eyes open anymore. The sofa looked inviting. He grabbed his coat and lay down, only to discover it was a good six inches too short. He tried to get comfortable but couldn't. Finally, he got up and made his way back toward the bedroom and climbed into bed. Maddy was still sleeping peacefully. He scooted closer, drawn by her smell and the warmth of her body. He longed to pull her into his arms, but he knew better. Instead, he tugged the blankets to his chin and closed his eyes. He felt himself drift off.

He was only vaguely aware of Maddy turning over. She inched closer and buried her face against the front of his sweatshirt. One hand came to rest on his crotch.

Michael's eyes shot wide open.

She moaned softly in her sleep. Her hand pressed closer.

Michael gritted his teeth. He could feel the warmth of her touch through his boxer shorts. Once again, his body sprang to life. She was still sleeping soundly; he could tell by her steady breathing. Her fingers reached inside the opening of his shorts and closed around his sex.

His self-control shattered. He was a dead man.

Michael sucked in his breath and prayed Maddy wouldn't wake up and come to her senses anytime soon. She began to stroke him ever so slowly. He closed his eyes and gave in to the sheer pleasure of her touch. Very gently, he slipped one hand beneath her pajama top and found her breast. He smiled when he discovered her erect nipple, and he wondered if she was having a sexy dream. She snuggled closer. He could feel her breath at his throat. Unable to resist, he dipped his head and pressed his lips against hers. Much to his astonishment, she parted her lips.

He snapped his head back. "Maddy?"

"Kiss me, Michael."

He didn't have to be told twice. Reclaiming her lips, he crushed her to him. The kiss was slow and thorough, his tongue gently exploring the petal softness of her lips. He had not forgotten how good she tasted or how sweet; yet it was like kissing her for the very first time. No, it was even better because he loved her.

Maddy lay there, head spinning, stomach swirling wildly as Michael's kisses turned hot and hungry. What in the name of heaven did she think she was doing? What had started out as something dreamy and intimately tender, a soothing balm for her tired and lonely soul, now threatened to burn out of control. She should put a stop to this madness, but each smoldering kiss sent a sweet ache through her body and left her craving more.

She felt Michael unbutton her pajama top and knew she was powerless to stop him. And when his lips appeared at her breasts, she closed her eyes and welcomed the warm gentle tug of his lips. As he teased each quivering nipple his hands massaged her breasts, sending currents of desire through her. His hair-roughened jaw grazed the tender skin and added to her pleasure. His touch was knowing and possessive, and Maddy's body responded eagerly. She felt transported to a soft and wispy place of feelings and sensations. Something coiled low in her belly, leaving her both anxious and eager for his next move.

Which is why she didn't protest when he removed her pajama bottoms and panties.

Michael stroked her thigh and smiled when he heard Maddy's breath quicken. He'd learned long ago where his wife was most sensitive, and he hadn't forgotten during their months of separation. He scooted down beneath the covers, skimming his lips from the valley between her breasts, across her stomach to her navel. Once there, he drew lazy, erotic designs with the pointed tip of his tongue that soon had Maddy squirming and moaning on the bed. He moved down farther still, his lips brushing past the springy gold curls that covered her mound. Very gently, he parted the folds that protected her femininity. Then, with that same patient, probing tongue, he searched for the small, sensitive bud that housed her desire. He knew he'd found it when she suddenly arched against him and plunged her hands through his hair. He inhaled her essence, the sweet musky scent of womanhood, and he tasted that most intimate part of her.

Unable to resist the pleasures that waited, Maddy opened herself to him. She would probably regret this night later, but for once in her life she was determined to enjoy the moment and let tomorrow take care of itself.

Michael's body responded immediately to her show of passion, and it was all he could do to bring himself under control. He felt hot all over; beads of moisture clung to his forehead despite the cold. Blood raced to his loins, filling him until he thought he'd burst from his need. He paused long enough to dispense with his shorts, then swept her legs open and positioned himself over her. He raised his head slightly, kissing her eyelids, the tip of her nose, her chin. Their breaths mingled.

"Maddy, I never thought we'd ever—"

She shushed him, placing a finger against his lips. She didn't want to think about what they were doing, didn't want to analyze it. "Don't say anything, Michael. Just love me."

He didn't have to be told twice. He entered her with one powerful thrust, sinking into her softness, filling her completely. The pleasure was beyond anything he'd ever known. "Don't move," he whispered, knowing he would explode if she did.

Maddy bit her bottom lip as she willed her body to lie still and feel him pulsing and throbbing inside. He kissed her, and his tongue made stabbing motions between her lips, sending erotic messages to the rest of her body and blocking all coherent thought. She arched high against him.

Michael cursed under his breath. Why did she have to feel so good? He plunged deep. She cried out softly and wrapped her legs around him.

Maddy climaxed twice before Michael finally allowed himself to let go. As he emptied himself into his wife he knew there was absolutely no way he was going to let her get away from him a second time.

Michael waited until Maddy fell asleep before leaving the bed to check the fire. He added a couple of logs and smoked a cigarette as he waited for the fire to take hold. In the semidarkness of the room, he continued to think.

He could feel his stomach churning with anxiety.

He was scared but hopeful.

They'd made love. That had to mean Maddy still cared.

Would she consider a reconciliation? If not, perhaps he could convince her to postpone the divorce long enough to see if they could work out the kinks in their relationship. They could still maintain separate residences if she preferred. He wouldn't rush her and risk losing her permanently.

Yes, that's what he'd do, talk her into waiting, say, six weeks, eight at the most. He would look for another job right away, one that didn't require him to put in seventy or eighty hours a week. They would start doing things together. They could take a vacation or maybe a second honeymoon. He would learn to like her dogs, especially Rambo, even if it meant buying a new pair of jeans every week.

They would discuss children.

He lit another cigarette. Children. Man-oh-man. He didn't know the first thing about kids. He could learn, of course. He could read books and watch videos and talk to the guys at work who had kids. If Maddy wanted a baby, then it was up to him to prove he could be a good father.

He glanced at his cigarette. He'd have to stop smoking. With Maddy being the health nut she was, she'd never permit smoking in the house with a baby around.

His mind made up, Michael tossed his cigarette into the fire, stirred it, and added a log. He hurried toward the bedroom, hoping to get a quick nap in before he had to get up and tend the fire again. He wondered how pioneers had ever managed to do all they did during the day when they'd had to get up so much during the night to tend the fire.

Maddy didn't stir when he climbed into the bed once more. He found her, much to his delight, warm and naked beneath the covers. He pulled her against him, nuzzled his face in her hair, and for the first time in months, fell asleep with a smile on his face.

Morning came much too quickly. Michael was jolted awake when Maddy's dogs jumped on the bed and pounced on him. Rambo shoved his long snout in Michael's face and growled.

"Hush, Rambo," Maddy said sleepily. When the dog persisted, she turned over to see what the problem was. Her jaw dropped open when she found Michael beside her. "What are you doing here?"

Michael thought she'd never looked prettier, with her hair tousled, her face flushed from sleep. "You invited me," he said, talking out of the corner of his mouth. "Hiya, Rambo." The dog snarled. "Has anybody ever talked to you about your morning breath, pal?" This time the dachshund showed his teeth.

"Stop teasing him," Maddy said.

"Teasing him? I was lying here perfectly still, minding my on business. I think your pet could use a lesson in manners."

"Rambo, get down!" Maddy ordered.

The animal refused to budge. Maddy sat up in bed, then shrieked and dove beneath the covers when she realized she was naked. "What did you do with my clothes?"

"I threw them on the floor next to mine," he said. "Don't you remember?"

Maddy opened her mouth to answer, but bit back her reply when Danny peered into the room. His eyes widened in surprise. "I was looking for Rambo and Muffin," he said. He glanced from Michael to Maddy, then to the pile of clothes on the floor. "Does this mean you guys made up?"

Michael was annoyed by the interruption. "If you want the dogs, come get them before Rambo takes my nose off."

Danny hurried over to the bed and grabbed both animals. "I added some wood to the fire," he said. "Y'all take your time. I know you have a lot of, uh, talking to do. I'll stay out of your way. Just pretend I'm not here."

"It would be a whole lot easier pretending if you weren't standing there gawking and flapping your jaws," Michael said.

Danny grinned and left the room, carrying a dachshund under each arm. It took some doing, but he managed to pull the door closed behind him. Michael climbed from the bed, unabashed in his nakedness as he crossed the room and locked the door.

Maddy was unable to tear her eyes away from the tempting male physique. For a man who was supposed to take off a few pounds, he looked surprisingly fit and sexy. His thighs and hips were lean and powerful, his chest still as broad as she remembered, and covered with thick, brownish-black hair. The sight of his partial erection made her tummy flutter. She blushed and looked away.

He climbed beneath the covers once more and reached for her.

"Michael, we need to talk," she said, trying to squirm out of his arms. It was like trying to squeeze through steel bars. "About last night—"

"Last night was wonderful," he said. "*You* were wonderful."

"Yes, but—"

He silenced her with a long kiss.

Maddy suddenly forgot what she was going to say.

As the kiss deepened, it was all she could do to think at all, much less provide an intelligent argument as to why they shouldn't be doing what they were doing. Michael nudged her thighs apart slightly with one hair-roughened knee and pressed against her intimately. She knew she was a goner.

Michael pulled the covers aside and feasted his eyes on her breasts. "God, you're beautiful. You take my breath away, Maddy."

She closed her eyes as he fastened his lips around one nipple. She shivered with delight and plunged her fingers through his hair. The muscles low in her belly seemed to contract with each gentle tug. "Danny's just in the next room," she whispered in warning, at the same time gripping his head, so tightly he wouldn't have been able to move had he wanted to.

Michael's reply was muffled. "He's got a whole stack of detective magazines."

"He might hear us."

"You weren't worried about that last night," he replied, moving to the other nipple.

Maddy blushed as she recalled the events of the previous night. What had come over her? Could it have been the wine? She seldom drank alcohol, maybe half a glass of champagne at a wedding, and even that much made her tipsy. The only reason she'd brought a bottle of wine to begin with was in case she had trouble falling asleep in a strange place.

No, the wine wasn't solely responsible for her actions the night before, even though it had left her feeling a bit amorous. She had simply been lonely and cold and craving human contact after months of having none.

"It was the wine," she said, deciding to use it as an excuse anyway, so he wouldn't think she lacked control.

He raised his head, and his gaze found hers. "Bull, Maddy. You knew what you were doing." He nipped the underside of one breast playfully, then kissed his way down her rib cage to her stomach. "Why not admit it— you were just plain horny."

She would have protested, but his tongue found her navel and her thoughts skittered to a halt. Talk about being putty in a man's hands. She gave new meaning to the phrase. Michael had only to give her that come-hither look of his, and she was lost. She moaned aloud when he swept her legs apart and covered her with his mouth. Once his tongue took possession, there was no going back.

Maddy arched against him and gave in to the sheer pleasure of his lovemaking. By the time he entered her, she was frantic to end the torturous need that had taken hold of every fiber of her being. She was surprised when he rolled over and pulled her on top.

Michael gritted his teeth as his wife tossed aside her inhibitions. Her body gripped his so tightly, it almost brought tears to his eyes. She exuded sensuality, with her wild blonde mane and her swaying breasts. Her head fell back, baring a slender white throat, and he raised one hand and stroked it with his index finger. Her climax was a thing of beauty, something to behold. Her lips parted softly, she whimpered, and as she coasted over the edge he felt her take a piece of his heart with him. His own orgasm was powerful and moving.

Michael could not remember ever feeling as content as he did at that moment, lying there with his wife in his arms. He adjusted the covers, taking care to see that she didn't catch a chill. He noted how quiet she was.

"Are you okay, sweetheart?" he asked, after a moment.

"I'm just tired," she said in a voice that seemed far away. "You probably don't remember but lovemaking always made me sleepy."

He pondered it. Now, what had made her say that? The Maddy he'd known had never wanted to rest afterward. On the contrary, she often jumped from the bed feeling happy and energetic. But he wasn't in the position to argue that point, since he was still pretending to have amnesia. It was probably safe for him to start remembering things now that they had reached this level of intimacy.

He weighed it in his mind. "Maddy, we should talk."

She yawned. "Can't it wait until after I take a little nap?" she said. "I suddenly feel very tired." She winced when her voice broke.

Michael raised up on one elbow and studied her, a perplexed look on his face. "Look at me," he said. When she didn't make a move to do so, he took her chin between two fingers and turned her head. Her eyes glistened with tears. "What is it, babe?" he said. "Didn't you enjoy our lovemaking?"

"Of course I did. How could I not? You were always an expert lover. I suppose you don't remember that either."

Michael stared at her in utter bewilderment. He wanted to gather her up in his arms, but the look on her face told him it wasn't a good idea. "Maddy, I don't like seeing you this way. Not after what we just shared."

"Please don't make a big deal out of it, Michael," she said. "Try to see it for what it was."

The muscles in his stomach tensed. "And what was it?" he asked, not sure he wanted to hear her answer.

"It was cold and dark, and I was scared we were all going to die before help arrived. I was reaching out for a warm body and someone to take my mind off my fears."

"And just now?" he asked. "What was that about? And don't tell me you were still scared."

"I was . . ." She paused and inched her chin higher. "Like you said earlier, I was just plain horny."

His mood veered sharply to anger. "Well, then. I'm glad I could be of service." He climbed from the bed and reached for his boxer shorts. "Perhaps you should visit one of those adult toy stores. They sell gadgets that'll take care of your sexual needs. You won't even have to say "I love you" afterward."

Maddy saw the hurt in his eyes and felt crummy for putting it there when the person she was really angry at was herself. She had let physical need get in the way of common sense. Now she would pay the price emotionally. Some people could sleep with another human being and not let their hearts get involved; she was not one of them. She could already feel the old wounds opening, gaping wide, leaving her as vulnerable to him as she'd been in the beginning.

"I wish you'd try not to get so upset over this," she said after a moment.

"Don't tell me how to feel, Maddy."

"Okay, be as upset as you like. It's *your* blood pressure."

"Oh, I get it. You just don't want to have to feel guilty when you cause me to have a stroke."

"If you have a stroke, it's not going to be because of me. Please hand me my pajamas," she said.

He crossed his arms over his chest and regarded her. "If you want 'em, come get 'em."

She glared at him, remembering with lightning clarity how angry he could make her when he put his mind to it. She had always felt things more passionately with him, and it irked her to no end that he still had that kind of power over her. As he stared back at her Maddy knew he would gnaw his arm off before he'd retrieve her things. She had committed the worst kind of sin, wounding that fragile male ego.

Giving a snort of disgust, she swept the covers aside and climbed from the bed. "This is so infantile," she said, marching over to where her pajamas lay. She could feel his eyes ravishing every inch of her, but she was determined not to let him know how much it bothered her. She leaned over and reached for her panties. Without warning, he smacked her hard on the bottom. Maddy gave an indignant squeal and whirled around. She was too shocked and angry to do anything more than sputter a mouthful of obscenities.

"Nice butt," Michael said, then strolled toward the door as though he hadn't a care in the world. He suddenly wasn't as mad as he'd been a few minutes earlier. She, on the other hand, appeared furious. She hurled a sneaker at his head, and he ducked. It bounced off the door. He let himself out and closed the door behind him, then cracked it and peered through the opening.

"You're going to have to watch that hair-trigger temper, Maddy," he said, trying to keep a straight face. "And I'd appreciate it if you didn't use that kind of language in front of the kid." He saw her pick up the other sneaker, and he closed the door quickly.

# NINE

Maddy came down the hall a few minutes later and herded her dachshunds into the laundry room to use their litter box. Once she'd disposed of the soiled papers, she washed her hands and offered them a doggie treat, all the while ignoring Michael, who waited beside the old percolator in his sweatshirt and boxer shorts.

"What happened to your jeans?"

"I gave them to Rambo. He was so attached to them, so to speak."

"Michael, that's ridiculous! He'll chew them to shreds."

His smile was chilly. He wasn't angry anymore, but he could feel himself getting depressed over his situation. "What can I say? The dog reached out to me in the cold, dark night, and fool that I am, I gave him what I thought he wanted. I'm just waiting for him to kick me in the teeth like someone else I know."

"Uncle Michael?"

"What?" He turned at the sound of his nephew's voice. The boy was holding his jeans.

"I found them in my sleeping bag this morning. They're a little wrinkled, and the hem is kinda ragged, but—"

"Thanks." Michael took the jeans from him and stepped into them. Once he'd zipped and buttoned them, he turned for the percolator and filled his cup. Maddy covered her mouth when she saw that a large part of the seat had been chewed out. Danny opened his mouth to say something, then glanced at his aunt, who shook her head.

Sipping his coffee, Michael walked to one of the windows. It was snowing lightly. Not enough to amount to anything, but he was sick of looking at it. He was sick period, but mostly he was sick at heart. What a fool he'd been to think Maddy would still have feelings for him. What a joke. He wondered what would have happened had she reached out during the night and found a stranger beside her. Would she have made love to *him* so wantonly?

He walked to the sofa and sank onto it. He was still sitting there staring into the fire when Maddy announced breakfast.

"I'm not hungry," he said, reaching for his coffee. He took a sip and was surprised to find it was ice-cold. The fire had died down as well, and he hadn't even noticed. How long had he been sitting there? he wondered.

"Go ahead and eat your oatmeal, Danny," Maddy whispered, rising from the table. She carried her coffee cup into the living room and sat down on the sofa beside Michael.

"I'm sorry if I hurt your feelings," she said. "It was not my intent. But you're going to make life miserable for the rest of us if you carry on like this."

He looked at her. She had showered and changed into black leggings and a fire-engine-red sweater. Her hair was tied back, drawing attention to her delicate cheekbones and a perfectly carved mouth. She was so damn pretty, it almost hurt to look at her. And to think, at one time she'd loved him as much as he loved her.

"How do you expect me to feel?" he asked, trying to keep his voice down so Danny couldn't hear.

"I'm not listening, Uncle Michael," the boy called out, "so you don't have to talk so low."

Michael sighed and shook his head and wondered why everything was going wrong for him. He started to take another sip of his coffee, remembered it was cold, and set it on the coffee table. "You've obviously lost all feeling for me," he whispered.

"What?" Maddy leaned closer.

"I said, you've lost all feeling for me." When she continued to look baffled, he almost shouted the words. "You don't give a damn about me anymore, Maddy! Did you hear that?"

"I've finished my oatmeal," Danny announced, shoving his chair from the table so quickly, it almost toppled over. "I'm going to read my detective magazines. I'll be in the bedroom if anybody needs me." He carried his bowl to the sink and whistled for the dogs. They followed him down the hall. He closed the bedroom door a moment later.

"He's being too nice," Michael grumbled. "I don't like it."

"Maybe he's learned a big lesson since running away."

He snorted. "Yeah, like don't get married."

"That's not fair to couples who've been happily married for many years."

"I don't have to be fair, Maddy."

"I really don't see what all the fuss is about, Michael. You don't even remember me. You don't know what flavor ice cream I like, you don't know what type of books I read, you know nothing about me."

This amnesia business was really beginning to work against him, he thought. But he couldn't conveniently regain his memory just because it had served his purpose for a time. He would have to start remembering things gradually, or she'd suspect the truth.

"I may have temporarily forgotten bits and pieces of our life together, Maddy, but my heart remembers. Why do you think making love to you last night and again this morning was such a natural thing for me? I seriously doubt either of us have ever shared that level of intimacy with another person. And you can give me that crap about being cold and reaching out to someone all you want, but you still feel something for me or you would never have given of yourself the way you did."

He stopped talking when he noted her bowed head and clenched fists. "What's wrong, Maddy?" He put a finger beneath her jaw and lifted her head so that he was looking directly into her face. Her eyes were bright and glistening with tears. They trembled precariously on her eyelids before falling to her cheek. "What's wrong, babe?"

She gulped back a sob. "Why are you doing this to me?" she cried. "Why are you punishing me?"

He shook his head. "I'm not trying to punish you," he said emphatically.

"You have no idea what it's like being married to a person who doesn't even know you're alive."

"That's not true, Maddy!"

"How do you know, you can't even remember how badly you treated me."

He gritted his teeth. How the hell could he defend himself when he was supposed to have amnesia? He stared back at her. "How badly I treated you?" he echoed. "Please be kind enough to fill me in."

"I don't want to talk about it." She started to get up.

He pulled her back down beside him. "That's too bad, because you're going to talk about it until I have a clear understanding of what a rotten husband I was to you. Now, then, did I cheat on you? Was there another woman?"

She sniffed. "No, it was nothing like that."

"Did I beat you?"

"Don't be ridiculous."

"I suppose I wasn't a good provider."

She was getting tired of his questions. "You were an excellent provider. We had everything we needed."

"I was a lousy lover, is that it?"

She glared at him.

"Surely, I did one nice thing during our marriage," he said, determined to make her remember the good times they'd shared.

She heaved an enormous sigh. "You attended a few plays with me," she said. "And a couple of artsy movies. You didn't enjoy them, but you attended anyway and never complained. Satisfied?"

"That's *it*?"

"You said name one, and I named two."

"If that's the only thing I ever did for you, then I'd want out of our marriage too."

"What's the point of all this, Michael?" She saw that he wasn't going to give up. "Okay, I suppose you want a blow-by-blow of every little thing you did for me. If that'll make you feel better, fine, but it's not going to make a difference to me because I've already decided what I want and don't want in life."

"Fair enough."

"Let's see now." She tapped a finger against her chin. "You always got involved in the charities I was interested in. You worked with me every year to collect food and toys at Christmas, and you hounded everybody at work to give. You always collected more money than anybody else when we walked for the March of Dimes. And you always gave blood, even though you don't like needles." She looked at him. "I'm sure I've missed something, but that's all that comes to mind at the moment. Let's suffice it to say you were a good neighbor to those in need."

He nodded thoughtfully. "Well, that's fine and dandy, but I was more interested in hearing if there were things I'd done for you personally."

She glanced away quickly. "Of course there were," she said, trying to sound casual about the whole thing. "I just can't remember them at the moment."

"Can't or won't?"

She didn't answer.

Michael stood and walked over to the fire. He grabbed the poker and stirred it, then placed a fresh log at the top. He continued to stand there and stare at the flames, wondering where their conversation was leading, afraid it might not lead anywhere. He couldn't force Maddy to love him any more than he could force to sun to come up in the morning. For someone who'd always needed to be in charge of his life and the situations around him, he suddenly discovered he was helpless. He could feel himself getting angry because of it.

"When my car's air conditioner went out last summer, you drove my car for a couple of days until it could be fixed. You didn't want me to have to deal with the heat."

Michael turned and looked at her. A single tear slid down her cheek. He wanted to go to her but didn't. He made himself stand still and keep quiet.

"And when I was hit with a really bad case of the flu a couple of years back, you stayed home with me for three days." She swiped at her tears. "You got so far behind at work that you couldn't take off when it was your turn to get sick."

Michael remembered she'd packed a thermos of soup for him each day during that time. And when he dragged home from work, she'd have a bath run, his pajamas laid out, and his cold medicine waiting. He'd climb shivering into bed, only to find the covers already warm from the electric blanket, and when he turned his nose up at food, she'd drive halfway across town for his favorite peanut-butter milkshake. He'd almost hated to get well.

He rejoined her on the sofa. "Sounds like we had a pretty good marriage, if you ask me," he said at last. "I can't believe you're actually wanting to divorce me."

"Believe it, Michael. You should have a copy of the separation agreement in your possession. That will offer you the proof you need."

"Speaking of the agreement," he said, clearing his throat. "You obviously haven't studied up on divorce laws in this state."

"I know that we have to be living separate and apart for one year before filing for a divorce."

"Separate and apart," he said, nodding in agreement, "and without resuming our marital relationship. You know what that means, don't you?"

His meaning didn't sink in at first, but when it did, Maddy felt the color drain from her face. They'd had sexual intercourse; they'd resumed their marital relationship. How could she have forgotten something like that!

The look on his face told her he hadn't forgotten. He was an attorney, and the amnesia obviously had not affected that part of his memory. He'd taken advantage of her neediness and voided the agreement completely.

She flew to her feet. "You slimeball!" she said. And just as she had begun to remember some of his more redeeming qualities.

"Now wait a minute," he said, standing as well. "*You're* the one who came on to *me* last night."

"You knew the consequences, you should have put a stop to it." She was angry enough to spit. "I should have done more than hit you over the head with that poker," she said.

He caught a brief image in his mind of what she would have liked to do. Half-afraid she might actually go for the poker again, Michael stepped between her and the wrought-iron fireplace tools. "You're getting upset, Maddy."

"Damn right I'm upset," she said, her look one of sheer hostility. "I don't want to have to start this whole procedure over. Can't you get it in your head, I don't want to be married to you any longer than I have to."

Her words sliced through him like knives. "Don't say things you might regret later."

She had begun to cry, but her tears were angry ones. "You want to know if there were good times in our marriage?" she asked. "Sure there were. When you were home," she added. "But you were seldom home, you see, so it wasn't much of a marriage at all. Most mornings I got up alone, I ate alone, and at night I went to bed alone. The only way I knew you'd come home was if you'd eaten the plate of food I left sitting on the stove or if you'd hung your wet towel over the shower door. And when Sunday rolled around and I dreamed of us doing something together, I'd always end up spending that day alone too. Finally, when I told you I just couldn't take it anymore, you told me to get a cat." She swiped at fresh tears. "Like that was supposed to make it all right."

"I'm sorry, Maddy."

"You didn't care about me, what was happening in my life or with my job. All you cared about were your clients and impressing the partners. I was nothing to you. I was just there to run your house and pick up your dry cleaning and take your phone messages. I figured I must be the worst wife in the world to make my husband prefer working eighty hours a week to coming home. Finally, I was convinced you were having an affair, and I started spying on you. I'd go through your wallet while you were in the shower or peek inside your briefcase. I even started listening in on your phone conversations."

She could barely talk through her tears. "That's when I realized I had to get help." She gave him a rueful smile. "I'll bet you never knew I was seeing a therapist, did you?"

He hadn't known any of it. He just looked at her, feeling as though his heart would break.

"It took several months for me to come to terms with the fact that our marriage was over. I had already begun looking for a place to live when I discovered I was pregnant." Her eyes took on a glazed look of pure anguish. "And I deeply regret that you don't remember the scene that followed when I told you."

He remembered. As badly as he wished he could forget, he suspected that memory would stay with him forever. "All I can do is apologize, Maddy," he said.

She picked up a pillow and hit him with it. "It's not enough. It doesn't even come close after you accused me of trying to trick you," she added, slamming him with the pillow again and again. "It never occurred to you that maybe I was so depressed over our crumbling marriage that I completely forgot to take my birth-control pills. You never once stopped to consider that I was just

as shocked and scared as you were." She hit him square
in the face.

Doing his best to dodge the blows, Michael finally
snatched the pillow from her. "Maddy, for God's sake!"
He grabbed her and she collapsed against him. She gave
a tortured cry that was followed by deep heartrending
sobs. Michael held her close, trying to offer what little
comfort he could. He suddenly realized his own eyes
were moist.

"They didn't even call it a baby when it died," she
said, her voice muffled against his sweatshirt. "They
called it a fetus, and they disposed of it as though it were
nothing more than waste material. I was supposed to go
on like nothing had happened. There was no grave,
nothing. No place to visit and take flowers."

Michael knew he should say something, but he
didn't trust his voice at the moment. He simply held her
in his arms and rocked her gently while she wept.
Danny came into the kitchen and grabbed a soft drink
from the refrigerator, then paused as though wondering
if there was something he could do to help. Michael
shook his head, and the boy hurried down the hall and
closed the door.

"Maddy, listen to me," Michael said. "You've got to
let go of these painful memories so you can go on with
your life. They're holding you back, sweetheart. And
you've got to let yourself forgive me once and for all."

She tore away from him. Her eyes were swollen, but
they were filled with accusation. "Forgive you?" she
said, as though the mere thought were too outlandish to
consider.

"Not because I deserve it, babe, but because it's doing harm to you to carry those feelings around. Surely, you can see that." She looked doubtful. "You can go on hating me for the rest of your life," he said. "But it's not going to change the past, and it's not going to bring our baby back."

She looked unmoved by his brief speech. "Sure, I'll forgive you, Michael. When hell freezes over." Without another word, she flung herself away from him and hurried down the hall.

Feeling dazed, Michael dropped onto the sofa. He waited until he heard the bedroom door close before he buried his face in his hands and sank into despair.

# TEN

When Michael finally raised up, he found Rambo lying at his feet and Muffin curled beside him on the sofa. Danny sat in the chair nearby, absorbed in a detective magazine. Michael patted the female dachshund on the head, and her brother wagged his tail and nudged his other hand so he could get attention as well. Half expecting the animal to try to take off his other thumb, but too miserable to care, Michael reached down and stroked him under his chin. Rambo surprised him by licking his hand.

"Well, now this is a change," Michael said. "I wish I could convince your mistress to like me."

Danny looked up from his reading. "You okay?"

"Yeah. I'm just worried about you. I've never seen you sit still for so long."

"This magazine is awesome, Uncle Michael. And it says these stories are true. I wonder if my dad has done any exciting stuff like they have in here."

"Oh, sure," Michael said. "Your dad's a regular

hero, only he doesn't like to talk about it. Your mother has told me some stories, though."

"Like what?"

Michael could see the kid was dying to know. He wondered why his brother didn't share things with his son. A boy should be proud of his father. "You know that dentist you see, that Dr. Graff?"

"You mean, Dr. Grafton?"

"Yeah, that's his name. Why do you think he never charges your family?"

The boy shrugged. "He told me Dad did him a favor once."

"Your dad did him a helluva favor. He was driving through Dr. Grafton's neighborhood one night, after somebody had called the station complaining about a barking dog. Actually, it was more like two in the morning. Anyway, your dad noticed the basement lights were on in a particular house, and he decided to check it out. He found the doctor, his wife, and three young kids tied up.

"At the time the city was still reeling over a murder that had taken place the week before, an elderly couple found shot to death in their basement. They'd been robbed. The two men seen leaving the scene of the crime matched the identity of the ones at the doctor's house."

Danny's eyes were wide. "Did anybody get killed at Dr. Grafton's?"

"Yeah. One of the burglars. Your dad didn't have time to call backup because one of the guys was holding a gun at the youngest kid's head. He thought it would be more fun if he started with the baby and worked his way up. Your dad knocked the window out, ordered the men to throw down their weapons, but this guy was determined to kill that little kid no matter what. Your dad took him out before he got the chance."

"He *killed* him?"

Michael nodded. "Shot the other guy in the hand and shoulder, pretty much put him out of commission till he could climb through the window and cuff him."

"How come he never told me?" Danny said. "I asked him one time if he'd ever killed anybody and he changed the subject. Sorta acted mad at me for asking."

"Cops don't like to kill people, Danny. Most of them will go to any length to prevent a shooting. But your dad wasn't about to let this guy take an innocent life, and I can tell you the Graftons never forgot it."

"He really is a hero," Danny said.

"Many times over," Michael replied. "Which is why he made detective before he was thirty. You have every reason to be proud of him."

"I'll bet my dad has better stories than the ones in this magazine," Danny said.

Michael could tell the boy was impressed with what he'd been told. "I'm sure he does. He's seen it all. Perhaps that's why he's so—"

"Strict?" Danny interrupted.

"Cautious," Michael said. "I guess when you've seen a lot of bad things in this world, you just naturally want to take special care of the people you love."

"Sometimes he goes overboard."

"Maybe now you'll understand why." Michael leaned closer. "Just think, Danny. Think what must've gone through his mind the night he saw those three kids tied up, a gun at the youngest's head. I'm sure it has stayed with him all these years."

Danny looked thoughtful. "He's going to ground me for a year because I ran away. I'll be eighteen before I have TV privileges again."

"Look on the bright side. You'll have more time to study. Your grades ought to be outstanding."

The boy gave him a cynical smile. "Thanks, that's just what I wanted to hear. Hey, one thing. How come I can't call you Uncle Mike?"

"Folks used to call me Mike. Then I went to law school and decided I was going to be this hotshot attorney, so I had everybody call me Michael. I thought it sounded more distinguished." He pondered it. "I think I liked myself better when I was just plain ol' Mike. It sounds solid. Unpretentious. I'd be proud to have you call me that."

"I'm sorry you and Aunt Maddy are having trouble."

Michael gave him the closest thing he had to a smile. "I guess it just wasn't meant to be."

"But you two belong together. Aunt Maddy's just upset over what happened in the past." He sighed. "I wish you could at least be friends."

Friends? Michael turned the word over in his mind as he tried to apply it to his and Maddy's relationship. True, they'd started out friends, but their feelings had quickly escalated, not only due to a strong physical attraction but a deep sense of caring as well. He wondered if it was possible to start back at square one with his wife. Friends. It wasn't what he wanted, but he had no choice if he hoped to maintain contact with her.

Of course, there was no guarantee that she'd even

want to be his friend after all that had transpired between them. He should never have tried to threaten her legally over the fact that they'd made love. It was low on his part, but it proved how desperate he was.

But Danny's idea might be worth a try. Convincing Maddy to be his friend would mean she would have to forgive him sooner or later. Once she forgave him and saw what a nice guy he really was, maybe she would consider something more.

If she even suspected what he was up to, she would toss him out on his head.

"You know, Danny. You just might have something there."

When Maddy opened her eyes, she discovered she'd slept later than she'd intended. No doubt she'd been exhausted after confronting Michael and crying so hard and for so long afterward. She felt empty inside, but strangely enough, she was at peace.

Even after months of pretending she was coming to grips with the loss of her baby and the disintegration of her marriage, she now realized she'd only been scratching the surface. She had refused to see Michael because she knew in her heart that she still loved him and could not face another loss. And she'd proved to herself just how alive that love was by inviting him to her bed the night before.

Yes, she loved him and pitied him. It had never occurred to her that he might have suffered over the loss of the baby. Even more so, because of the way he'd reacted to the pregnancy. She had clearly seen the anguish in his eyes, and now she felt utterly miserable knowing she hadn't tried to comfort him in some small way.

She had expected too much from her husband, and she knew it was because her parents had ignored her for most of her life. She'd been determined to prevent the same thing from happening in her marriage. She had resented his job and everything else that had taken him away from her.

Maddy knew it was time to own up to her share of the blame where her marriage was concerned. For not being proud of her husband when he came to her after winning a particularly difficult case. For shunning the other lawyers' wives who tried to involve her in so many of their activities. She'd preferred being alone and miserable because she'd hoped to make Michael feel guilty. Which was why she hadn't left him a message the day she'd miscarried. She knew he would feel terrible when he found out she'd had to go through it alone.

Maddy could feel her heart constricting inside—she was not proud of the things she'd done or the person she'd become. How Michael could make love to her as he had, how he could possibly want to be with her, that was something she didn't understand. Of course, he'd lost his memory. He might not want her back once he remembered what a witch she'd been.

Maddy felt a surge of fresh tears. She had wasted ten months of her life and Michael's, feeling sorry for herself and blaming him for her unhappiness. It was time she took responsibility for her feelings. Michael was not a court jester hired to make her smile and be happy all the time.

She thought of the way he'd humbled himself before her and asked her forgiveness.

She should have been asking his.

She should have confessed her true feelings, told him how much she still loved him, begged on bended knee for a second chance.

Maddy's heart leaped to her throat as she considered it. A second chance? Would he even consider it once she told him the truth?

She jumped and dragged the blankets to her chin when somebody knocked on the door, as if by doing so she could hide her sins as well. She swiped hot tears away as Michael stepped in with a tray, looking more wonderful than any man had a right to. How had she ever convinced herself she would be better off without him? Why hadn't she tried harder instead of giving up and going into hiding?

Michael smiled tentatively. He could tell Maddy had been crying, and his heart felt heavy. "I hope I didn't wake you," he said. "Danny and I warmed up some soup for lunch. I thought you might like a bowl."

Her smile was tremulous. "Thank you," she said, embarrassed to have him see her with her eyes red and puffy. He set the tray on her lap.

"Mind if I sit for a minute?" he asked, indicating a chair near the bed. "I need to tell you something."

Her heart skipped a beat. It was bad news; she could tell just from looking at him. He'd discovered what a shrew she was, and he was going to try to escape down the mountain because he preferred death to being trapped in the cabin with her. "There's something I have to say as well," she said.

Michael felt momentarily panicked as he dragged the chair closer to the bed. Was she going to tell him all the things he didn't want to hear, that she was finished with him and never wanted to lay eyes on him again? He couldn't bear it, his only hope was to convince her otherwise by following his new plan of action.

"May I go first?" he asked quickly. When she hesitated, he went on. "What I have to say won't take long."

She nodded and tried to prepare herself for the worst. "I'm listening."

"Well, I've had a few flashes of memory in the last couple of days and . . ." He paused at her look of surprise. "I didn't want to say anything until it was completely restored. Hopefully, I'll be good as new before long."

Maddy scooted farther beneath the blankets.

"Anyway, I remember the part about me working a lot, and the problems we had because of it. I was selfish to put you last."

She suddenly realized which direction he was going in. "Michael, I've something to tell you." She wasn't about to let him take the rap when she was equally to blame.

"Please let me finish," he said, then smiled meekly. "Otherwise, I might not have the courage."

She waited. It must be bad.

He cleared his throat. "What I want to do is apologize, from the bottom of my heart, Maddy, for all the times I've let you down. I never meant to hurt you, I just wanted to give you a better life than my own mother had and . . ." He paused and raked one hand through his hair. "Well, I knew your parents were filthy rich and that you'd had every advantage growing up. It kind of embarrassed me when they just up and bought us a luxury condo without even discussing it with us. Not that I wasn't bowled over by their generosity, you understand, but I sort of sensed they thought I couldn't take care of you."

She shook her head. "Oh, Michael—"

"True, I can't give you the things they gave you, but I figured once I paid off my college loans, we'd start looking for a nice place."

"Michael, I don't even like that condo."

"You don't?" He looked surprised.

"Why do you think I asked you to stay and try to sell it? Besides, my parents didn't buy it because they were afraid you couldn't provide for me. They bought it out of guilt. It's their way of making up for not being there while I was growing up. For letting the servants raise me."

"Why didn't you tell them?"

More tears. Lord, she had cried enough of them this day. "Because I didn't want to seem ungrateful. And because I've never been able to stand up to my parents or tell them what I needed from them. They were always so glamorous. People flocked to them. It was like living with a couple of celebrities." She shrugged. "I guess I was intimidated by them," she added. "But not anymore. I've learned I have to assert myself if I hope to get what I want in this life."

He was quiet for a moment. He knew he had to come clean with her on a certain matter before he tried to put his plan into action. If she ever decided to give him a second chance, which seemed doubtful at the moment, then he was going to have to take all pressure off of her. The decision would have to be hers and hers alone. Made without pressure or duress.

"Maddy, about the separation agreement. I misled you. No judge is going to toss it out on an isolated incident of sexual intercourse. The agreement is still in full force. I just told you that because I thought I could buy a little time. But after hearing how miserable you were with me, I realize I don't deserve it." He could feel the sweat beading on his brow. That one had cost him a lot. And had surprised Maddy as well. "I just want you to be happy, Maddy. Even if it means living without me."

She didn't say anything. She was too busy trying to pull herself together.

Michael moved the chair to its place in front of the window. He turned, swallowed hard, and went on. "Before we were lovers, before we were husband and wife, we were friends. It was a friendship I cherished, Maddy, and one I'd like to keep, if at all possible."

"You're willing to be friends and nothing more?"

He knew he was being tested. He saw the funny look on her face and suspected she wasn't falling for it. He had to try harder. "Yes," he said solemnly. "I've come to terms with the fact that our marriage is over, but I can't come to terms with losing your friendship. I need that part of you in my life, Maddy, and I'd like to think you need that part of me. I'd like to be the one you call when you've had a bad day, or one of your parents gets sick, or if you lose someone dear to you. Like when you lost Mr. Yates."

Maddy wasn't sure she was hearing right. "Sort of like a big brother?"

He almost blew it by groaning out loud. The last thing he wanted was for Maddy to think of him like a brother. "More like a best pal."

She tried to hide her disappointment. "Well, that's certainly a nineties way of thinking," she said, trying to sound casual.

"And you can call me Mike."

She arched one brow. "Mike?"

He offered his hand. "What do you say? Friends?"

Maddy wasn't quite sure what to make of the situation, but she shook his hand anyway.

"You didn't eat your soup," he said. "Danny and I might have to drag you out in the snow and throw snowballs at you."

Maddy forced a smile to her face that she did not feel. He was teasing her, but there was no intimacy, as there had been before. Friends. "Would you, uh, mind taking it for now, uh, Mike?" she said, testing the name on her tongue. "I'll warm it up later."

He didn't argue with her as he would have under normal circumstances. He simply picked up the tray and headed for the door. "Danny found a deck of cards. You're welcome to join us in a game of poker. We're using toothpicks."

"Thanks," Maddy said. "I think I'll read."

She watched him go. Feeling heavyhearted, she fell back on the bed and stared at the ceiling for a long time, trying to come to terms with what they'd just agreed on.

She wouldn't cry. She'd felt sorry for herself long enough; that was part of the problem. She would hold her head high and go on with her life, because she knew, with or without Michael—uh, Mike—she was responsible for her own happiness. And if friendship was the only thing he wanted from her, that's exactly what she'd give him.

Danny was sitting at the counter with his detective magazine and a deck of cards beside him when Michael carried in the tray containing the uneaten soup. The boy put down the magazine and began shuffling the cards.

"Well?" he said.

Michael joined him at the counter. "I think she bought it. I'm not sure she agreed with it, she'd probably rather wash her hands of me all together, but she went along with it."

"So what's the next move?"

He paused. "Well, I guess I'll have to treat her like a friend from here on out. Just one of the guys, so to speak."

"Yeah, right," Danny said, rolling his eyes. "First time she comes prancing through the cabin in those tight thingamajigs she wears—"

"They're called leggings."

"—and those clingy sweaters, your tongue will drop to the floor, and you'll be right back where you started, following her around like a puppy dog." He thought for a moment. "I've got it! We could burn them in the fireplace while she's sleeping."

Michael frowned. "Whoa, Danny boy. That's a bit extreme, isn't it? I mean, we need pretty things to look at while we're up here with no amusements. Besides, what's she going to think when she wakes up and all her clothes are gone?"

"We can tell her we were robbed during the night. 'Course, that means we'll have to ransack the cabin and burn all our clothes too. We'll pretend we slept right through it. Oh, and we'll have to take turns walking around in the snow out front so there'll be tracks leading to the door. Once we get rid of all those cute little things she wears, you won't be at her mercy anymore. Got it?"

"I can see those detective magazines have really got you thinking, but don't you agree that it's going to look strange that someone broke in and took our clothes but left the food and blankets behind?"

"Oh, yeah."

"Besides, Maddy isn't going to have time to do any prancing around tomorrow, because I'm going to put into gear my new emergency-preparedness plan, which is not only going to impress the hell out of her, but make her realize she can't live without me."

"Cool. What are you going to do?"

"*We*, Danny. We're all in this together. It's time to get ourselves prepared in case help doesn't arrive for a while. There's going to be a lot of hard work involved, so I'm counting on you."

"Hard work?"

"First thing we'll need to do is carry in all the wood from the shed." He grinned. "And there's a lot of wood back there, my friend. Your Aunt Maddy's going to be right in the thick of things. And you know why? Because she's—"

"One of the guys," they said in unison, and gave each other a high five.

Danny seemed to ponder it all as he dealt the first hand. "Do you think anyone knows we're up here?"

"I'm sure of it. Your dad would have reported it right away. Problem is, nobody is going to bring a chopper through these mountains with zero visibility. Which is why I haven't bothered sending up flares."

"How long you think we'll be up here?" Danny asked.

Michael didn't wish to frighten him. "Oh, it shouldn't be too long. But it's always wise to take precautions."

When Maddy entered the kitchen sometime later, she found Michael stirring something on the stove. She checked the pot. "Beans?" she asked.

"Beans. You'd be hard-pressed to find a healthier food. I seem to have bought a case of them." He glanced at his nephew. "Hit the showers, Danny."

The boy saluted and made his way down the hall.

"I've been meaning to ask why you would buy an entire case of pork-and-beans," Maddy went on. She peered into the box. "Never mind, I just got my answer."

"What?"

"All the cans are bent."

"Is that a problem?"

She couldn't help but smile. "You'd buy boots with no soles if they were discounted. Shirts with no buttons if they were cheap enough. You probably don't remember the time you bought a whole side of beef because the price was good. It didn't matter that we had no place to store all that meat and ended up buying a freezer that very night so it wouldn't go bad. That side of beef ended up costing us three times what it was worth."

He leaned against the counter and regarded her. "So, you're saying I'm cheap." He knew he had a tendency to shop for bargains—he got it from his mother who'd almost had to work magic to cover the bills and feed a family of seven on a policeman's salary. Meals consisted of beans and rice, inexpensive casseroles, and day-old bread. They'd had powdered milk that left an aftertaste, but the Kelly children were expected to drink three glasses a day nevertheless.

There'd been no such thing as air-conditioning in their house, and homework had been done at the kitchen table, where the only light burned after dark. If you happened to be taking a bath, you had to bathe in six inches of water, two and three at a time. Clothes and shoes had been purchased once a year, and the wearer had to take care of them because that was it till summer.

If you had a job and could afford to buy your own, you were lucky. Even so, half the money from those jobs had gone into an account. There had been no such thing as fun money. Michael often wondered if Maddy would ever be able to relate to such a life.

"I wouldn't exactly call you cheap," she said, after a minute. "Let's just say you tend to be tightfisted at times." She chuckled. "Actually, the whole incident with the side of beef was pretty funny. I was thankful you hadn't run into a good deal on a live cow."

Michael couldn't help smiling as he remembered the

two of them jumping in his car and racing to the nearest appliance store, only ten minutes before closing. The owner, a broad-chested, cigar-smoking man, had told them they couldn't buy the floor model just because it was already cold inside, and that he absolutely could not have the freezer delivered until the following day. Michael had simply written him a check and handed him a hundred-dollar bill, and that had been that.

Later, once they'd loaded the shanks and steaks and roasts into the freezer, Maddy sat on the floor tallying what Michael's latest bargain had cost them, and she'd laughed until she'd lost her breath. He'd decided the only way to shut her up was to lie on top of her and cover her mouth with his. They'd made love on the living-room carpet.

They were quiet for a moment, and Michael wondered if Maddy was remembering. He hoped so. For every bad memory she had, he knew there were three good ones. His job was to point them out, subtly. In the meantime he would carry on this good-buddy relationship and hope she realized how much she missed the deep bond they'd once shared. As independent as she preferred to be, he still believed in old-fashioned relationships between a husband and wife.

He wanted to take care of her, even though he knew she was capable of taking care of herself. He wanted to protect her, with his own life if he had to, and he wanted to be there to catch her if she fell, even though the likelihood of that happening was slim.

"How about I make some rice to go with your beans," Maddy said, breaking into his thoughts. "I don't usually like serving more than one starch per meal, but I think I can make an exception here, since we'll need something that sticks to the ribs. And I'll slice a couple of tomatoes to go with it."

Michael nodded. "Good idea. By the way, does your watch have an alarm?"

She shook her head. "No, but I have my small travel alarm clock with me. Why?"

"I need to borrow it. So I can set it to wake me every hour and tend the fire. Otherwise, it goes out, and the whole place gets cold."

"Oh, Michael, I'm so sorry. I didn't even think. I don't mind taking turns with the fire. You have to get your rest or you'll collapse."

He wished she wouldn't use that tone of voice with him because it made him want to curl up next to her and never get up, and that's not the way their relationship was supposed to be working right now. Friends. Pals. Good buddies. He hoped she would begin to want more after a time.

It wasn't easy thinking of her as just another Joe. Just as he seemed to get his body under control, she went and did something utterly cruel, like bend over to pick something up or put fresh water down for those dogs of hers, and he was forced to stare at that pert behind while trying to breathe calmly so he didn't hyperventilate. And what about that business of snuggling her dachshunds against her breasts? What was *that* all about? Sure, she pretended she was just playing with them, but he knew what she was doing. She was purposely trying to draw attention to her body.

He only wished he could think of something to drive *her* out of her mind.

Maddy noted his deep frown. He was a million miles away. "Michael, are you even listening to me?"

"Huh?" He glanced up, realizing she'd caught him gazing off into space again. "I'm sorry, I was just thinking . . . and planning . . . for any emergency that might crop up." He knew she liked his chest. He could walk around without his sweatshirt. Of course, it would be cold as blazes, and he would probably get sick as hell, but it would be worth it.

"Okay, enough is enough," Maddy said. "As your friend, I insist that you stop worrying immediately." She snapped her fingers. "How about a glass of wine? That'll relax you. You can sit in front of the fire and drink it while I finish dinner." She grabbed the bottle from the refrigerator and poured him a glass. "There now, that should do the trick." She set it on the counter beside him.

A noise overhead made them look up. "What was that?" Maddy said.

"Well, Santa and his reindeer aren't scheduled for another month, so I have to assume a tree limb fell on the roof. Which reminds me, I'd better climb up there tomorrow and see what it looks like."

"Wait just a minute," she said. "If you think I'm going to stand by and let you climb up on an icy roof, you're crazy."

Aha, she was worried about his safety. Definitely a good sign. And one way for him to prove how courageous he was. "Calm down, Maddy," he said. "I know it's dangerous but—"

"Dangerous is right. You could fall right through

that roof and put a big hole in it, and then where would we be? We'd all freeze to death in an hour."

Michael felt the spark of hope fade.

"Hey, look what I found in the attic," Danny said, coming down the hall with a large metal object in his arms.

"Attic?" Michael said, glancing at Maddy, who shrugged. "That must've been the noise we heard. Guess I won't have to go up on the roof after all."

"It's a space heater," Maddy said excitedly. "I wonder if it works? Plug it in, Danny. No, wait. It might have a short. Let Uncle Mike plug it in."

Michael shot her an icy look, but took the heater from the boy and carried it to the nearest outlet. He plugged it in and the coils instantly lit up. Maddy and Danny clapped.

"Where on earth did you find this attic?" Maddy asked.

"It's in the roof of your closet. I went in there to get clean clothes and felt this spiderweb, so I shined a flashlight around, and saw this thing that looked like a trapdoor. I dragged a chair over and stacked your suitcase on it, and there I was."

"What else did you find up there?" Michael asked.

"A bunch of old newspapers and books. Oh, and some more detective stories. Can I go back up?"

"I don't know, Danny, it might be dangerous," Maddy told him. "The wood could be rotted in places."

"Better let me go," Michael grumbled. "If there's any danger involved, your aunt will want me right in the middle of it."

Maddy tried to hide her amusement. "Michael, that's not how I meant it to sound."

"And if you should have a hankering to drink Red Devil lye and set yourself on fire with gasoline before dinner, please let me go first so I can check the level of danger."

"Michael, what a thing to say," Maddy said, chuckling. Danny grinned.

"Now, if you'll excuse me, I'd like to run a bath and drink my wine, since Danny's more interested in exploring than showering the way he was supposed to." Michael grabbed his wine and turned for the hall. "Maddy, did you want me to check the wiring on your blow dryer while I'm in the tub?"

She remained straight-faced. "No, thank you. You'd probably end up dropping it in the water and ruining it."

# ELEVEN

When Maddy came into the kitchen the following morning, she found all the groceries on the counter and Michael and Danny making lists. "What's going on?" she asked.

"Oh, hi," Michael said without looking up. "We're taking inventory of the food. There's another storm on the way. No telling how much snow we'll end up with or how long before we get out of here. I'm afraid we're going to have to start rationing food."

"Don't you think that's a bit extreme?"

"Not in the least. And since I'm in charge, that's the way we're going to do it." He winked at Danny, who smiled in return. He would show Maddy he could handle their newly formed friendship, despite being in love with her. He would also prove he was capable of taking care of her and keeping her safe. A tall order, but he was up to it.

One blonde brow lifted high on Maddy's forehead.

"Mind telling me who put you in charge, Mike, ol' buddy?" she asked.

"Danny and I voted on it."

"And I didn't get to vote because . . . ?" She waited.

"Because you refused to get out of bed when I knocked on your door earlier."

"Was that *you* banging on my door at the crack of dawn?" she said.

"Yes. You were obviously more interested in sleep than in saving your life."

Maddy stared back at him. He was up to something; she could feel it in her bones. She would love to know what it was. She regarded him quizzically. "Okay, since you've put yourself in charge, I think it's only fair to tell me where you received your survivalist training. Now that you hold my very life in your hands," she added.

He put down his pen and looked up. "I have my instincts. Not only that, I'm bigger, stronger, and a whole lot—"

"Don't even say it," she warned, holding up one finger. "If you wish to keep all your body parts intact, stop right where you are."

Michael knew the flashing green eyes meant business.

"If you don't believe he's the strongest, you should try and arm-wrestle him," Danny said, jumping to his uncle's defense. "Besides, he's the only one carrying a weapon."

This surprised Maddy. "You have a weapon?"

Danny answered for him. "Yeah, an awesome bow and arrow. It's in his car."

Michael nodded. He'd excelled in archery as a Boy Scout. His parents had bought him a nice bow when he'd received his Eagle Scout badge. He only hoped he could remember how to use it after all these years. "I figure if the food gets low, I'll hunt."

"Knowing the proper use of a bow and arrow doesn't necessarily make you a wild-game hunter," Maddy said, still smarting over the fact that they hadn't let her vote.

He grinned. "The best we can hope for is that I run into an old arthritic bear who's on his last legs and can't outrun me."

"Well, if you think I'm going to eat some poor bunny rabbit or brown-eyed doe that you slaughtered in cold blood, right in the middle of the holiday season when we're supposed to be kind and giving, you've got another think coming. You've always been against hunting."

"I can't imagine killing an animal for sport," he said. "But if I have to kill something to keep us from going hungry, I will."

"You're overreacting, Michael. The plow will come up these roads any day now."

"Let's hope you're right. In the meantime I'm going to take every precaution."

Danny looked at Michael. "Can I take a short break and play with the dogs? I've got writer's cramp."

"Be back at 0900 hours."

Danny saluted. "Aye aye, Skipper."

Michael ruffled his hair. "We're not in a boat, pal, but you can call me Skipper if you like." Danny grinned and took off down the hall. He closed the bedroom door a moment later, and Rambo barked his greeting.

"And what am I supposed to call you?" Maddy said.

"You may refer to me as O, Great One," he said. When she didn't even crack a smile, he slapped her on the back. "Just kidding, Maddy. Besides, you've probably already picked out a name for me anyway." He winked. "Now, how about some coffee? I put salt in it just like you do." He grabbed a cup from the cabinet and filled it, then added cream and sugar.

"I hope it's not too salty," he said as she raised it to her lips.

Maddy took a sip and knew she'd made a bad mistake. She immediately spit it in the sink and filled a glass with water.

"Too much salt? I used the smallest measuring spoon I could find. I only had one cup because of my blood pressure. Still, I hated to throw it out."

When she could talk, she turned to him. "Let's make a deal," she said. "You just worry about keeping us alive, and I'll take care of the coffee situation."

"But I get up earlier than you."

"I'll set it up the night before. That way you'll only have to plug in the percolator when you wake up." She poured the coffee down the sink and prepared to make a new pot. She saw Michael wince. "It's not a sin to waste it under these circumstances, O, Great One. Even your mother would have given her blessing."

He knew she was insinuating he was cheap. Coming from Maddy, he didn't mind it. "My mother would have let it cool and watered her plants with it."

"Perhaps it hasn't come to your attention yet, but

we have no plants. Perhaps that's why we call you O, Great One instead of O, Wise One."

"Maddy?"

She paused at the sink. His voice was odd, yet gentle. She turned. He wore a thoughtful smile. "Yes?"

"You're okay, you know that? I'm even going to like you after the divorce."

She knew he meant it as a joke, but the pain that knifed through her was anything but funny. She swallowed, and it felt as though a bowling ball were lodged in her throat. "That's what all my ex-husbands say," she replied lightly. "Would you excuse me?"

Maddy hurried down the hall to the bathroom and locked herself inside. Once the tears came, they gave no hint of subsiding. She sat there for a good twenty minutes, trying to bring herself under control. She'd thought she had it licked. Indeed, she assumed she was ready to embark on a new life. But she only had to take one look at her husband and spend one night in his arms, to know she was right back where she started.

And now, now that she knew what was in her heart, he was ready to back off, be a friend and nothing more. He was even joking about their upcoming divorce.

Maddy was startled by a quick knock at the door and Michael calling out to her. She quickly washed her face and opened it.

His expression was bleak. "Oh, Maddy, why am I such a thoughtless SOB? I don't know what came over me. We were having fun one minute, and I just blurted out that business about the divorce without thinking."

Maddy drew in a ragged breath and managed a tremulous smile. "It's okay, Michael. Really."

He placed one hand against her cheek. "I'm not good enough for you. I never was."

"Oh, please don't start that," she said, rolling her eyes and ducking out of the bathroom. She made her way to the kitchen and finished making the coffee, then plugged the percolator in. Michael sank to his knees and grabbed her from behind. "I'm not even good enough to breathe the same air you breathe."

With him still grasping her, she turned, and it was all she could do to keep from bursting into laughter. This was how every single argument they ever had ended, with Michael pulling his shenanigans and her falling into fits of giggles. They usually ended up in bed, still laughing over it.

"Michael, stop it this instant," she said. "You're a grown man and a respected attorney, you can't keep acting like this. Besides, you're supposed to be preparing for this catastrophic snowstorm, remember?"

"I'm not even good enough for you to wipe your feet on. But go ahead anyway." He fell to the floor on his stomach, trying to spread himself out so she could do as much walking and wiping her feet as she liked. He stacked one fist on top of the other and propped his chin. "Go for it, Maddy."

"You are certifiably crazy, you know that," she said, standing on his broad back. "Okay, Michael, I'm wiping my feet on you. Do you feel better now?" She glanced up and found Danny standing a few feet away, wearing the same look he had the night she'd hit his uncle over the head with the poker and slammed the door.

"Uncle Michael! What's she doing to you?"

"Huh?" Michael turned his head. "She's . . . uh
. . . well, it's hard to explain, kiddo."

Maddy wondered if they'd managed to warp the
kid's mind for life in just a few days. "The ol' skipper
threw his back out, honey," she said. "Good thing I
know how to fix these problems."

"Is it serious?"

She looked thoughtful. "Hard to say without a rectal
thermometer, but after a quick examination, I'd venture
to say your uncle is suffering from spondylosis."

"What causes it?" Danny asked.

"Old age, honey. Your uncle is over the hill, so to
speak."

Michael turned his head so that he could see her.
"Very funny, Maddy. And we both know you don't need
a rectal thermometer to diagnose back trouble."

She smiled sweetly. "No, that's just something extra
I like to do for my patients."

"Is he going to have to lie there like that?" Danny
asked.

"Oh, no. The only chance for a cure is heavy exercise. And he'll have to sleep on a board. Preferably one
with nails in it."

"Maddy, would you please get off my back now,"
Michael mumbled.

"Ah, the coffee is finally ready," she said, stepping
off and making her way to the percolator. "Would you
like a cup, Mike?"

His smile was brittle. "I think I'll fix it myself. Then
perhaps we can get back to the business of discussing my
emergency-preparedness plan."

Rambo and Muffin began barking from the bedroom, obviously missing their playmate. Danny started in that direction.

"They have to use their litter box first," Maddy said.

"I'll take it back there," Danny offered, already going into the utility room. When Maddy started to protest, he interrupted. "I know how to do it, I've watched you. Don't worry, I won't throw up."

"Well, that's certainly comforting," she said. Once she was situated at the counter with her coffee, she glanced at the food lists. "You need to give me the job of rationing food and preparing the meals," she said. "I'll be able to stretch the food while seeing that it meets our nutritional needs."

"Fine. Danny and I have enough to keep us busy." When she began rolling up her sleeves to get to work, he stopped her. "First things first, though. We have to bring in the wood from the shed so it can start drying."

"Okay. I'll finish this inventory while you guys do that."

"Sorry, Maddy. We need every available hand we can get."

"There are only two pairs of wading boots," she pointed out.

"I noticed you had a pair of boots with you when I unloaded your car."

She gave a snort. "And you expect me to wear those to lug wood back and forth in the snow. I don't think so. They're genuine crocodile boots from the Congo basin in Zaire, Africa, where my parents recently traveled to see old friends. They paid a king's ransom for them. They're lined with lamb's wool, and if they get wet, they'll be ruined. I refuse to destroy a perfectly fine pair of boots in this snow." She sighed. "Oh, God!"

"What?" Michael looked startled.

"I sounded just like my mother."

Twenty minutes later everybody was suited up. "Hey, nice boots, Aunt Maddy," Danny said. "My sister has a pair just like 'em."

"I seriously doubt—"

"Hers are lined with lamb's wool. Are yours?" When Maddy ignored him, he went on. "And right inside there's a stamp that says 'Made in Africa.'"

Maddy could feel Michael watching her, but she refused to meet his gaze.

"What do you have on under your clothes?" Michael asked her.

"I beg your pardon?" Maddy said, taken aback by the personal nature of the question.

"We've got a twenty-degree-below windchill factor out there, and the wind is whipping through like a typhoon. I want to make sure everybody is warm enough. It's better if you layer your clothing."

"I've got on two of everything," Danny volunteered.

Both man and boy looked at her, as though sizing her up. "I'm perfectly capable of dressing myself warmly," she said. They started for the door. "Uh, Mike, ol' buddy?" she called out.

He turned and offered her an easy smile, determined not to let her see how this friendship thing was grating on his nerves. "Yeah?"

"You didn't tell us what you were wearing under *your* clothes."

"That's the luxury of being in charge, missy. I don't have to answer to anybody."

"On the contrary. Our survival depends on your survival. You've put yourself in charge because you felt you were more qualified. I, for one, have not seen anything to indicate as much, and since I wasn't permitted to vote, I think I have every right to question whether or not you're taking necessary precautions to stay healthy. And please don't cal me missy. Unless you want me to call you by some of the cute little pet names I've given you over the years when you were feeling amorous."

Danny looked at his uncle. "What did she say?"

Michael's gaze locked with hers, but he could feel the heat creeping up his neck and spreading across his cheeks at the thought of his nephew learning the names he'd earned in the bedroom. The woman had no shame. "You want to know if I'm prepared?" he demanded. He closed the distance between them and met her gaze. There was a feral quality to his look. "If you'll step in the next room, I'll be more than happy to accommodate you," he said silkily. "But I'll expect the same courtesy."

"Are you guys fighting again?" Danny asked in a bored voice.

Maddy could tell by Michael's tone that she was treading on dangerous ground, and she didn't want to give her nephew yet another sideshow. "Never mind," she said.

"May we proceed?" he asked.

Maddy followed Michael outside, and the wind almost slapped her to the ground. She saw that Danny was having trouble standing as well. With Michael leading the way, they staggered toward the woodshed.

Maddy's eyes watered from the cold, and her ears ached. She wondered if their caps and gloves offered enough protection. The cold seemed to knife through her jacket and jeans, despite the thermal underwear and sweatshirts she wore beneath them. Her fancy crocodile boots were slippery in the snow and much too tight with two layers of socks, but she knew it would have to do.

The shed was in shambles, worse than when Maddy had first arrived, and the firewood was buried beneath an avalanche of snow and rotted wood. Working as quickly as they could, they spent several hours pulling away pieces of the collapsed roof so they could get to the firewood below.

It was slow, agonizing labor, and Michael insisted they go inside every fifteen minutes to warm up and place their mismatched gloves before the fire to dry. They lunched on canned soup and grilled-cheese sandwiches and went back to work.

As the afternoon wore on, Danny began to complain, and at one point he became so belligerent, Maddy asked Michael to send him in. But he refused to coddle Danny, even when the boy seemed to be deliberately dragging his feet. Maddy tried with all her might to remain upbeat, but she knew she couldn't take much more.

"Okay, I'll finish up out here," Michael said. "You two go inside and get warm." When Maddy started to object, he waved her off. "I won't be long, go on."

The wind seemed to have picked up. As Maddy and Danny made their way toward the front door of the cabin, she had to hold on to him to prevent him from stumbling. At least he'd stopped complaining.

Inside, she tore off her hat and gloves and helped Danny do the same. "I know you're exhausted, honey," she said, once they were out of their coats. "But you have to get out of these wet things." She helped him off with his wading boots and sneakers and pulled his socks off. She'd handed him dry clothes from in front of the fireplace and told him to put them on. He nodded.

"Would you like to go ahead and get your bath first?" she asked, noting the boy could barely hold his eyes open.

"After I rest."

"Don't forget to put your wet things in front of the fire," she reminded him. "Once I clean up, I'll make you a cup of hot chocolate." She hurried down the hall.

Maddy wasted no time running a bath. The old claw-foot tub and pedestal sink would have been pretty, if she'd hired someone to reglaze them as she originally planned. As it was, they were chipped and discolored but still serviceable. She loved the deep tub, and as she filled it with water she added her favorite lavender-scented bath salts.

Maddy sighed her immense pleasure as she lowered herself into the tub, letting her poor tired muscles and quivering flesh absorb the heat from the water. She leaned back and closed her eyes. A good soaking would go a long way toward lifting her mood and lowering her anxiety level. At least she hoped so. There was nothing quite as stressful as being trapped under the same roof as your soon-to-be ex-husband, especially when you were still in love with him.

What made it so much worse was the crazy way Michael was acting. How could he make mad, passionate love one minute, insist on a platonic relationship the next, then treat her as if she were in boot camp? If she didn't know better, she'd think he was doing it all to confuse her. He was succeeding very nicely.

Maddy had been in the water less than ten minutes when Michael banged on the door.

"Time to clear out, Maddy," he said. "Danny and I need to grab a shower while there's still hot water."

"I'll be out shortly," she said, not giving it a second thought.

"This is no time for prissing around," he told her. "The rest of us need to clean up too."

She glared at the closed door. The man was really beginning to annoy her and test the limits of their so-called friendship. "I just got in here, for Pete's sake! I refuse to let an entire tub of hot water go to waste."

"You've got five minutes."

Maddy gritted her teeth. Just who the hell did he think he was, telling *her*, a grown woman, how much time she could spend in the bathtub? It was absurd, especially since Danny was sound asleep and had no desire to bathe at the moment.

He was doing it for spite. Had he been nice and asked her in a polite tone of voice instead of using his drill-sergeant routine, she might have reconsidered, but he could go jump in a frozen pond for all she cared. She'd sit there till next spring if she liked.

Michael was back in five minutes. "Maddy, get the hell out of the tub now! Something's wrong with Danny."

# TWELVE

Wearing only her panties and bathrobe, Maddy leaned over her shivering nephew and tried to get a response from him. "Danny, can you hear me?" He mumbled something incoherent, then drifted off. She began taking his pulse.

Michael paced nearby. "I got worried when I couldn't get him to wake up," he said. "Why is he still in his wet clothes?"

"I gave him dry clothes to put on," she told him, "but I couldn't very well stand there and *watch* to make sure he changed."

"I'm not blaming you, Maddy. I'm just worried. He looks very sick."

"His pulse is too slow," she said. "He's got hypothermia, Michael. I don't know how severe it is." Her eyes watered. "I should have suspected something by the way he was acting. He staggered in like a drunk. Please help me get him out of these clothes. First, let me plug that electric heater in. We need all the heat we can get." She dragged it to the nearest outlet and turned it on high.

Working as fast as he could, he pulled off Danny's jeans and the sweats he wore beneath them. The boy didn't even try to protest, but his teeth chattered non-stop. Michael finished undressing him and turned to Maddy, who stood as close to the fire as she dared, frantically warming towels and T-shirts, and the sweats Danny normally slept in, in front of the fire. She tossed Michael a towel, and he dried the boy while she dragged two ladder-back stools from the kitchen and placed them near the fire. She draped a blanket over them to absorb the heat.

"Why don't we just set him in a tub of hot water?" Michael asked.

"That could make things worse." Together, she and Michael dressed the boy in thermal underwear and sweats, plus a pair of Michael's socks that had been lying on the hearth for some time. "See if those towels are warm enough," she said.

Michael nodded and handed them to her.

"Okay, you're going to have to lift him so I can place the towels beneath him." He did as he was told. Once Maddy had them in place, Michael lowered the boy gently. She grabbed another towel from the hearth and wrapped it around his head and neck like a turban.

"What's that for?" Michael asked.

"To hold in the body heat." Next, she covered the boy completely with the blanket, tucking it all around him.

"He's still shivering."

"That's okay. I'd be more concerned if he suddenly

stopped." She looked at Michael. "I didn't like the way his fingers and toes looked. Did you notice?"

"They were awfully white."

"It might be frostbite."

"Oh, that's just dandy. My brother's going to appreciate the way I took care of his kid."

"You didn't do anything wrong. Besides, we can't worry about that now," she said. "There's too much to do."

"What do you want me to do?"

"We'll need more towels and blankets warmed up. Just drape them over those stools. I think I brought my hot-water bottle; you know how I pack everything I own when I go someplace." She started out of the room. "See if you can wake him, get him to talk to you."

Maddy hurried down the hall toward her bedroom and located the oversized tote bag that contained what essentials she'd thought she would need for a trip to the mountains. She dumped the contents on the bed—two cosmetic pouches, her bath salts and oils, creams and lotions, her blow dryer and curling iron, and finally her hot-water bottle and a heating pad. Nobody could ever accuse her of not being prepared, she thought.

She reached for them, upending a half-open box of tampons. Any other time she would have paused to pick them all up, but she was more concerned with her nephew than anything else.

She hurried into the bathroom and waited for the water to warm up for the hot-water bottle. Not too hot, she reminded herself. Once she had the bag secured, she made tracks for the living room. Michael was talking loudly to Danny, as though his hypothermia and frost-bite had rendered him deaf.

"I pledge . . . allegiance . . ." Danny's words were slurred. His teeth chattered. He drifted off.

Michael nudged him gently. "To the flag."

"The flag."

"Come on, Danny, I know you can say the Pledge of Allegiance."

"Of the 'nited States of 'merica."

Maddy slipped the hot-water bottle at Danny's feet and propped it with a pillow so it would touch his toes. After locating an extension cord, she plugged in the heating pad, turned it on low, and placed it on Danny's chest beneath the blanket. Then, using extreme care, she lifted his small frozen hands from his side and placed them directly on the pad.

"With liverty and just for all," the boy finished.

Maddy looked up. "Liverty?"

Michael looked at her. He could tell she was scared. So was he. But they had to keep their heads, or they wouldn't do Danny any good. "This is not the time to be picky. Once he rests up a bit, I'll have him sing 'The Star-Spangled Banner,' how's that? Just kidding," he said, when her mouth dropped open. "Would you calm down? You're making me a wreck."

Maddy took a deep breath. Adrenaline was still pumping through her body after the scare and all the racing about she'd done. She looked at Michael. "I don't know about you, but I could use a cup of coffee."

"I'll make it while you put some clothes on," he said. "I don't need two sick people on my hands." He also didn't need to keep seeing that robe flap open each time she turned, giving him a clear shot of long shapely legs. He had enough to think about

"Michael?"

He glanced up. "Yes?"

"Leave off the salt?"

He smiled wearily. "Okay, but only because you asked me nicely."

Maddy dressed in her pajamas and put on thick socks before she stuffed her feet into her bunny slippers. Her dogs, who surprisingly enough had slept through all the ruckus, now raised theirs heads and yawned wide, each emitting a squeaky-door sound that always made Maddy chuckle.

"Do we need to potty?" she said. They both stood and wagged their tails and followed her to the utility room. Once they'd taken care of their business and Maddy had cleaned up the litter box, she checked on Danny. He was still shivering, though not as badly, and he opened his eyes when she touched his cheek.

"Rambo and Muffin miss you," she said softly.

He turned his head slightly and gazed at the two dachshunds. He smiled, then he looked at Maddy once more. "Am I sick?" he asked, still talking through chattering teeth.

"You got too cold out there today, honey," she said.

"My fingers and toes hurt."

"You also got a touch of frostbite. Nothing serious," she added quickly, not wanting to frighten him. "I can give you a couple of aspirin if you like. Do you think you could swallow them?" He nodded, and she smiled. "Tell you what, I'll make you some hot cocoa too. That'll help warm you up."

"I already beat you to it," Michael said, when she entered the kitchen. He poured a pan of hot water into a cup of cocoa while she got Danny's aspirin and water.

Michael gently held Danny up so he could take the medicine and sip the cocoa. "We might as well change the towels and blanket," he said. "While we have him up."

"I'd rather go ahead and pull out the sofa bed," Maddy told him. "If you could just hold him for a minute." Michael picked up the boy, and she tucked the blanket more securely around him so he wouldn't get cold.

Michael carried Danny to the chair and sat down, holding him in his arms as he would an oversized infant. As he gazed at his nephew he knew he'd never have been able to live with himself if something had happened to him.

A groggy Danny opened his eyes. His smile was weak. "Are you going to sing me a lul'by, Skipper?"

Michael felt something sting the backs of his eyes. He blinked. "Yeah. When pigs fly." He voice came out sounding gruff, but the look in his eyes was one of love and deep concern.

Once Maddy had made up the bed and placed the warm towels in the very center, Michael laid the boy down. Maddy put the heating pad on Danny's chest and placed his hands on top, then covered him with two freshly warmed blankets. She fashioned a towel around his head like before, then checked his hot-water bottle to see if it was still giving off enough heat.

"What do you think?" Michael said quietly as they sipped their coffee in the kitchen.

"He's going to be okay. You and I need to sleep with him tonight."

"On the sofa bed? Won't that be kind of crowded?"

"That's the point. He can absorb our body heat. Besides, I don't want to leave him for one minute, and we can't risk letting the fire burn out."

"I should never have forced the two of you out in this cold," Michael said, his expression guilt-ridden.

"Stop blaming yourself. We all dressed warmly and took every precaution. Children are more susceptible to hypothermia because of their size, and Danny's on the skinny side to begin with." She reached over and covered his hand with hers. "He's going to be okay." She suspected they would probably take turns reassuring each other over the next twenty-four to forty-eight hours.

"How about you?" he asked, suddenly looking anxious. "Do you feel okay?"

"I'm perfectly fine. And Danny will be too."

But Michael couldn't stop worrying. While Maddy prepared dinner he kept the fire going and sat on the edge of the sofa bed, watching for any sign of improvement. The boy had finally stopped shivering, and he seemed to be sleeping peacefully, but still, Michael fretted. In the past, when he'd thought of children, he'd viewed them as a hardship, what with buying clothes and shoes, feeding and educating them, the costs for medical and dental work, and a whole slew of other expenses. He'd sympathized with his colleagues who were parents, who sometimes had to sit up all night with a sick child, only to have to go to work come morning. Now he realized just how lucky those people were to have someone in their lives who loved and needed and trusted them.

He no longer pitied them, he envied what they had.

"Michael?"

He jumped when Maddy called his name. He hadn't even heard her come into the room. She stood there holding a steaming bowl. He saw the concern on her face, but this time it was aimed at him.

"Why don't you take a break while I try to get Danny to take this broth," she suggested.

"I'll feed it to him." He woke the boy gently. It took some convincing, but they finally got him propped up on several pillows so Michael could spoon the broth into his mouth.

Maddy checked Danny's toes and fingers and saw, to her relief, some of the color had returned. Nevertheless, she refilled the water bottle and put it in place.

"How do you feel, Dan-the-Man?" Michael asked, teasing the boy.

"Tired. I just want to sleep, but you guys keep bugging me."

"It's for your own good, buddy. You gave us a scare, and you're not out of the woods yet."

Once Danny had taken about half the broth, Michael pulled the pillows from beneath him and exchanged his blankets for two that had been warming in front of the fire. As he tucked them around the boy Danny opened his eyes briefly.

"Thank you, Uncle Mike, for taking care of me."

Michael had never seen his nephew look so trusting, and the emotion was as powerful as if he'd just received a blow to the chest. "You're welcome, kiddo."

They sat up late, warming towels and blankets and feeding the fire. As though sensing something was wrong with Danny, Muffin and Rambo jumped onto the sofa bed and curled up at his feet.

It was after two A.M. when Maddy and Michael finally decided to lie down, each of them pressed close to Danny. As Michael draped a protective arm over the boy, he discovered Maddy had done the same. He touched her hand, and they linked fingers. Minutes later they had dozed off.

Michael wasn't sure what woke him the next morning, but he opened his eyes with a start and sat straight up. He automatically glanced over at Danny and found the boy awake. Maddy was sleeping soundly on her side of the sofa bed. "How're you feeling, champ?" he whispered.

"Hungry."

"I'll make you something," Michael said, taking care to speak quietly. "Let your Aunt Maddy sleep as long as she can. She was up a lot during the night."

They both had been up and down much of the night. Michael had seen to the fire, since he didn't trust the electric heater and had finally unplugged it. Maddy had kept towels and blankets warming so that Danny wouldn't risk getting chilled. Several times she'd made the boy drink something, although he had complained and insisted he was too tired. The sky had already begun to lighten when they'd finally given in to exhaustion.

Michael glanced at his wristwatch and saw that it was after ten o'clock. He climbed from the bed quickly, knowing he had a lot to do. It wouldn't be easy trying to write a message in the snow with broken tree limbs, but that's all he had to work with. He would spell out the word *medic* in great big letters, then send off his flares and hope for the best.

And once they'd packed and were waiting for help to arrive, he would call Maddy to the bedroom and have a final heart-to-heart conversation. He'd learned a lot about life during the past ten months; even the last few days had been an eye-opening experience for him. If nothing else, he now knew what was important to him and what wasn't.

Danny insisted on sitting at the kitchen counter to eat his oatmeal, although Michael draped a warm blanket around him and set the heater nearby. He sipped his first cup of coffee and watched his nephew anxiously while Maddy slept on.

"Uncle Mike?" Danny said, speaking just above a whisper.

"Yeah?"

"Do you think Aunt Maddy's going to stop the divorce?"

The man shrugged. "I don't know, Danny. But I don't want you worrying about it. You need to concentrate on getting better."

"I could try to talk to her for you and tell her what a good person you are. I mean, look what you went through for her, all that planning. You even pretended to have amnesia for her."

Michael quickly glanced toward the sofa bed to make sure Maddy was still asleep. She hadn't so much as turned over. Poor thing was probably exhausted.

"You know the good thing about being sick?" Danny said. "My parents probably won't come down on me as hard for running away."

"Does this mean you've scrapped the idea of hitching a ride up to Canada after all?" Michael asked, looking amused.

"Remind me never to tell Aunt Maddy my secrets," Danny said.

"She loves you very much. You 'bout scared her to death when you told her your plans."

Danny shrugged. "I figure Canada can wait. I'm kinda in a hurry to get back home."

Michael heard a noise from outside and wondered if that's what had awakened him in the first place. He hurried to the window and looked out. He was both relieved and disappointed to find two snowplows heading their way. For Danny, who needed to be checked by a doctor, it was good news. As for him, he would be too busy packing and getting the boy ready for the trip back, and probably wouldn't have time to talk to Maddy the way he'd planned.

His time was up.

Maddy heard the noise, too, and knew what it meant. She'd been lying there quietly, listening to the fire and the sound of her nephew's voice. He still sounded a little weak, but he was on the mend. It lifted her spirits. Then, just as quickly, they sank.

Michael had faked his amnesia. He'd made a fool of her. What made it worse was that Danny had known. Oh, how the two of them must've laughed over her naïveté. When had Michael become so cruel?

He had played her like a tune. He'd gained her sympathy; she'd given her heart and body.

But she'd always been a fool where her husband was concerned.

No more.

Planting a cheerful smile on her face, Maddy climbed from the sofa bed and joined the two in the kitchen for her first cup of coffee. She wouldn't waste time fighting with Michael. She just wanted to pack her things and get out.

Besides, there was no reason to fight. They were finished.

# THIRTEEN

They packed in record time. Michael waved down one of the heavy-equipment operators and paid him fifty dollars to pull Maddy's Jeep out of the ditch. They were on their way, once he threw things in the car and put the fire out.

The trip down the mountain was slow; here and there he found patches of ice, despite road crews working to put sand out. Michael constantly watched his rearview mirror to make sure Maddy was following close behind.

The hospital was located in the foothills, a sprawling one-story building on the edge of town, blanketed by snow. Michael carried Danny into the emergency room, where a young intern saw him right away. Maddy found a comfortable chair and sat quietly in the waiting area while Michael paced.

"Are you okay?" he asked her. She hadn't said more than a dozen words since they'd arrived.

"I'm tired and I'm worried about Danny," she said,

keeping her voice neutral. She leaned her head back and closed her eyes, hoping he would take it as a hint that she needed rest more than conversation.

As for his question, she wasn't okay. She was hurt and angry. Why had Michael let her think he was more seriously injured than he had been? Why had he pretended to have amnesia? She couldn't figure it out for the life of her. Then it came to her like a lightning bolt and made her angrier. He had sought to gain her sympathy and make her feel guilty, hoping she would treat him kindly instead of throwing him out like he deserved. And she had played right into his hands, seeing to his every need, beating herself up emotionally for hitting him with that poker.

She had been used.

*And* she had made the monumental mistake of sleeping with him, not once, but twice. Worse than that, she'd fallen in love with him all over again.

Correction. She'd never fallen *out* of love with him.

But she was too tired and worried about Danny to get into a discussion with Michael. She just wanted to know that her nephew was going to be okay so she could go back to her life. And once she got her divorce, she would leave town if she had to in order to keep from seeing Michael again.

"Mr. and Mrs. Kelly?" Maddy's eyes snapped open and she sat up straight as the young intern approached them.

Michael stopped pacing. "How is he, Doctor?"

"Your nephew is going to be fine. I'd like to commend you on your sharp thinking in an emergency situation. Danny told me what the two of you did, and I would have done the very same thing under the circumstances."

Michael looked at Maddy and smiled. "My wife is the one who told me what to do. If it had been up to me, I'd probably have sat there wringing my hands all night."

Maddy was deeply touched by the pride she saw in Michael's eyes, but she glanced away quickly, not wanting to be caught up once again in conflicting emotions. "What about the frostbite?" she asked the intern.

"Luckily, it was mild. He's almost fully recovered. In fact, he asked me for directions to the nearest fast-food restaurant." He smiled. "You two can stop looking so worried now. Danny's free to leave as soon as his discharge papers are in order. I understand he's feeling a little homesick."

"May I see him?" Maddy asked.

"Sure. Oh, Mr. Kelly, if you want to come with me, I'll show you where you can sign him out. You may want to call the boy's parents for insurance information."

Michael nodded. "I was planning to call as soon as I knew something."

Maddy stepped into a small cubicle a moment later, where she found Danny dressed and in a hurry to go. "I understand you're hungry," she said.

"Yeah, I'm going to order a double cheeseburger and large fries and maybe a milkshake. Where's Uncle Mike?"

"He's calling your parents to let them know you're okay. As soon as you're discharged, you can go." She suddenly felt a lump in her throat. "I came in to say good-bye, honey. I checked on Muffin and Rambo once, but I'm afraid to leave them in the car much longer."

"Aren't you going to Mickey D's with us?"

"No, sweetie, I'd better get on back." She leaned forward and kissed him on the forehead. "I'll call and check on you in a couple of days."

"Don't forget to put in a good word about me to my mom."

"Of course. That's what aunts are for." She hugged him. "I love you, little buddy." She turned quickly so he wouldn't see the tears in her eyes.

"Hey, you've got to hang around long enough to say good-bye to Uncle Mike."

"I would appreciate it if you would do that for me." She left before he had time to respond.

When Michael came into the room sometime later, he was wearing a grin. "The good news is you're going to live. The bad news is your mother and sister are going to drive you crazy over the next few days waiting on you hand and foot."

"What about my dad?" Danny tensed as though expecting the worst.

"He was on his way out to buy ice cream and all the detective novels he could find."

"So he's not mad?"

The smile disappeared from his face. "I'm not going to lie and tell you he wasn't disappointed, Danny. I did tell him what a trooper you've been the past few days, though. Maybe he'll go easy on you."

"There goes any hope of getting a driver's license before I'm forty years old," the boy mumbled.

Michael wasn't listening. "Where'd your Aunt Maddy go?"

Danny hesitated. "She left."

"Left the hospital?"

The boy nodded. "Said she was in a hurry to get back."

"I need to try and catch her," Michael said, turning for the door.

"She's been gone fifteen minutes, Uncle Mike. She asked me to tell you good-bye for her."

"Good-bye?" Michael simply stared at the boy, feeling as though he'd just been punched in the gut.


The offices at Smyth-McGraw bustled with activity. As Michael waited to be admitted into Gray Smyth's inner sanctum, he wondered how Danny was doing. He missed the kid. He'd rented a video during lunch and planned to take it by later so they could watch it together. He hoped Brenda would have news from Maddy.

The pain was still raw. Why had Maddy left without telling him good-bye in person? Surely, he deserved better than that after the last harrowing night they'd spent together. After everything they'd shared.

And here he'd thought she still had feelings for him, that maybe, just maybe, he was getting that second chance he'd hoped for all these months. What a fool he'd been.

"Mr. Kelly?"

Michael looked up. His boss's secretary stood before him. "Mr. Smyth will see you now."

Gray Smyth's office was papered in a deep hunter-green fabric and furnished in camel-colored sofas and chairs with smart piping around the cushions that gave them a rich, dressy appearance. His desk was solid teak-wood, a gift from his grandfather, one of the founders of the firm. Always the gentleman, Smyth stood and offered Michael a handshake, then motioned him to sit in one of the leather chairs facing his desk.

He was a distinguished-looking man with salt-and-pepper hair that should have started thinning decades ago but hadn't. His suit was silk, only the best. They chatted briefly about a case Michael had been working on while Smyth's secretary brought them coffee on a silver tray.

"I know your time is valuable, sir," Michael said, "so I'll get right to the point." He pulled an envelope from his pocket and handed it to the man. "It's my resignation, Mr. Smyth."

The man shook his head sadly. "Are you unhappy with the firm, Michael?"

"No, sir. I'm very much impressed with Smyth-McGraw. But I'm afraid the long hours have caused me to ignore my health, and as a result my blood pressure is way up. There's also my family to think about."

"I'd heard you and your pretty wife had separated. I know the long hours can take a toll on even the best marriages."

"I hope to rectify that situation, sir, as well as my health problems, but it means rearranging my priorities."

"But we have our own gym, Michael. And a cafeteria that can accommodate any diet."

"I haven't exactly had much time for either, sir. Not with my current workload."

Smyth opened a side drawer and pulled out a folder. "I was afraid something was up so I asked personnel to send me your file. You've given this firm everything you had to give, and you're one of the best damn attorneys we've got. I'm not a stupid man, Michael. I know our competition would love to have you, and I know you've been contacted by them in the past. Is that what this is all about? Did one of them finally get to you?"

"I haven't accepted a job with another law firm, Mr. Smyth, but when I do, it won't be with another big firm. I'll probably go out on my own or with a single partner."

"And you expect me to be happy about that?" Smyth said. "Knowing our men will have to face the street fighter in court?" He paused. "What's the bottom line here, Michael? What's it going to take to change your mind?"

Michael hadn't expected this. "I beg your pardon?"

Smyth leaned back in his chair and smiled. "You've been listening to stories on how good the senior partners have it, haven't you? Well, it's true. Once you leave the trenches, so to speak, the workload drops dramatically. You're suddenly surrounded by secretaries and paralegals and eager young lawyers willing to work all night if they have to in order to make you happy. You get to eat in the fancy dining room with the other bigwigs, and you usually make it home in time for dinner each night. And weekends . . ." He smiled. "When's the last time you had a whole weekend to yourself?"

Michael tried to remember. "Well, except for a couple of holidays—"

"On top of all those benefits, your salary is increased and you get a cut of the profits. What do you say?"

Michael blinked. "About what, sir?"

"You know, you come across much brighter in court, but I imagine I took you by surprise. I'm offering you a promotion and raise and all the other glamorous things I mentioned. You would have made senior partner in another couple of years anyway, but your record speaks for itself. Unless you'd rather go find a dirty hole in the wall so you can start your own practice, and let your poor family starve to death while you're trying to drum up enough clients."

Michael was so stunned, he didn't know what to say at first. "I truly wasn't expecting this, Mr. Smyth. May I have a couple of days to think about it?"

"Of course. I can certainly see why you'd feel torn. By the way, may I have your wife's address?"

Michael was embarrassed to tell him he didn't know it. "I'll have to get back to you on that," he said. "Why do you ask?"

"Should you decide to accept the promotion, I'd like to send her flowers and thank her for all the sacrifices she's made because of your career." He winked. "The wives eat it up."

Dr. Joseph Quigley smiled the minute he walked into his exam room and found Maddy Kelly sitting there. "And here I thought it was going to be another dull day treating flu patients. What can I do for my favorite gal?"

Maddy's eyes automatically teared. She had promised herself she wouldn't cry, but she couldn't seem to help it. "I need a pregnancy test," she said.

"Oh?"

"Don't give me that innocent look, Dr. Quigley. I know you sent Michael to the mountains for some R and R because of his blood pressure, right about the time you suggested I go instead of imposing on my friends at Thanksgiving. And with a snowstorm on the way. Wait till I tell Sylvia you've been sticking your nose in your patients' business again."

He became defensive. "How was I to know you'd really go? My patients never listen to me. By the way, Michael's blood pressure dropped considerably."

"And I'm two weeks late for my period." The tears fell in earnest as she remembered unpacking her bags at home and seeing the unused tampons. She was supposed to start shortly after Thanksgiving. "You know I'm never late."

He reached for the box of tissues. "Could it be stress-related?"

She snatched several tissues from the box and tried to mop her eyes. "Not even stress makes me late."

"Well, I don't mind giving you a test, hon, but why didn't you just buy one of those do-it-yourself kits?"

She gave him a grim smile. "I had a hankering to see you."

"That's understandable, me being a strapping young doctor with a sporty Volvo station wagon."

She sniffed. "The other reason is because I'm not that late. I was afraid one of those over-the-counter tests wouldn't be accurate. I understand the most accurate way to find out is a blood test. I called my OB-GYN, and I can't get in till next week. I have to know now."

"Well, hon, I can take the blood test, but I've got to send it to the lab. Even if I put a rush on it, I won't get the results until tomorrow afternoon. Do you think you can wait that long?"

Maddy was already rolling up her sleeve.

The following day, Maddy was doing paperwork at her desk when a strange man holding an elaborate vase of flowers knocked on her door.

"Mrs. Kelly?" he asked.

She nodded dumbly and watched as he set them down.

"Oh, and there's a letter with it," he said, pulling an envelope from his shirt pocket. He handed it to her.

Maddy noted the return address and wondered why Smyth-McGraw would send her flowers. She waited until she was alone before she opened the envelope.

*We at Smyth-McGraw are proud to announce your husband's recent promotion to senior partner at our law firm. We know you will join us in congratulating him for all the hard work and effort he has put in to earn this prestigious title. We are holding a small breakfast, two weeks from today, to officially welcome Michael into the fold, and to thank you for the sacri-*

fices you've made over the years for his career. Please
call my secretary for details.

Cordially yours,
Gray Smyth

Maddy picked up the phone and called Brenda.
"What am I going to do?" she asked, once she'd read
the message to her sister-in-law.

"I don't know, Maddy," the woman said. "Does
anybody at the firm know you and Michael are separated?"

"I'm sure word has gotten around by now."

"Well, you don't want to do anything to jeopardize
this promotion. And it's very nice of the firm to include
you in the celebration as well. How many companies
take the time to send the wife flowers acknowledging
her participation in her husband's career? Do you think
the department ever thanked me for all the nights I sat
up worrying myself silly when I knew darn good and
well my husband was involved in a dangerous assign-
ment? Heck no."

"You're right," Maddy said. "I have to be there. Will
you be seeing Michael between now and then?"

"Are you kidding? I can't seem to get rid of the man.
He either calls or visits Danny every day. He helps him
with his homework, then they go to the gym. All those
workouts are helping Danny with his self-confidence.
Oh, and Michael has even baby-sat the girls a couple of
times. You ask me, I think you should have hit him with
that poker a long time ago."

Maddy sighed. "Well, when you see him, would you
please tell him I'll be at the breakfast."

"Sure, honey. I think you're making the right decision."

"Don't go getting the wrong idea," Maddy said. "I'm doing it for his job."

"Right. I understand."

As Maddy hung up the telephone she couldn't help but wonder if she was making yet another mistake where her husband was concerned. Seeing Michael again would only cause her pain and anguish. And she was still madder than a hornet over the amnesia business. But it was only fair that she do this one last favor for him, since she knew how hard he'd worked. His career was his life.

It was his wife, mistress, and best friend.

But she had another reason for wanting to be there as well. When all was said and done, she wanted to be able to look in his eyes and see if he thought his success was worth what he'd given up.

The phone rang, and Maddy snatched it up. The woman on the other end introduced herself as an employee from Knell Laboratories. "The results of your blood test were positive, Mrs. Kelly. Dr. Quigley asked me to call as soon as I knew."

Maddy sat in stunned silence. "Are you sure?" she asked.

"I have the results right here in my hand."

Her head was spinning. "And this test is accurate?" Maddy asked. "One hundred percent accurate?"

The woman on the other end chuckled. "Honey, the only thing you can count on more than this test is planning for the day you bring that baby home from the hospital. If I were you, I'd start knitting booties."

# FOURTEEN

Maddy's absolute joy at being pregnant dimmed a bit a week later when she awoke with her first bout of morning sickness. Once it passed, she cleaned herself up and stumbled into the kitchen for the box of soda crackers she planned to keep on the nightstand beside her bed from that moment on. Unfortunately, the nausea didn't abate. It was still with her when she looked up from her desk that afternoon and found her sister-in-law standing in the doorway of her office.

"Brenda, what are *you* doing here?"

"We had a lunch date, remember?"

Maddy glanced at her desk calendar and saw that she was right. "Oh, I'm so sorry. Yes, of course, we did." She stood and rounded the desk.

"Are you sure you're up to it?" Brenda asked. "You don't look so good. I hope you're not getting that awful flu bug."

"No, I'm fine." Maddy reached for her purse.

Brenda grabbed her jacket from a brass coat tree

beside the door and tossed it to her. "Here, you'll need this. Oops."

In an attempt to catch her coat, Maddy dropped her purse. Brush, comb, wallet, sunglasses, ink pens, and soda crackers scattered in a dozen different directions.

"I'm sorry," Brenda said, kneeling to help pick it all up. She reached for the crackers and handed them to Maddy. "Upset stomach?"

Maddy blushed. "Yes, I think I have a stomach virus."

"Does Michael know?"

Maddy shook her head, not trusting herself to speak.

Brenda grabbed her hand and dragged her out of her office. "Let's cruise."

Fifteen minutes later they were sitting in Brenda's car at the park, lunching on cheese and crackers, cold milk, and canned peaches.

"It happened at the cabin, of course," Maddy said. "It was late, and I was cold and—" She paused. "It was my fault."

"The way you talk, one would think you'd committed a crime."

"We're going to be divorced next month, Brenda."

The other woman turned in the seat so that she was facing Maddy. "When are you going to stop this nonsense and realize the two of you belong together?"

Maddy shook her head. "If you had heard the things he accused me of last time. If you'd seen how he acted toward me."

"Maddy, do you think my darling husband hasn't disappointed me before? Oh, you ask him and he'll tell you he's Mr. Wonderful, and I'm lucky to have him, but believe me, he can also be Mr. Pain-in-the-Butt. Why, I've been mad enough to shoot his tires out with his own gun. One time I packed his bags and called his mama to come get him. Kathleen refused, of course. Said I was stuck with him. One day that woman is going to need a favor from me, and I'm going to remind her of that night."

Brenda paused while Maddy laughed. "But I learned early in our relationship that I couldn't hold grudges. Not if I was going to be married to a man with a dangerous job. And let me tell you this. If you think Michael won't disappoint you again in this lifetime, then you're wrong. Men can't help themselves. They say and do stupid things, and it's up to us to be wise and forgiving."

Maddy found herself smiling. "I've missed you."

"I haven't been anywhere, dear."

"I know. I didn't come around because I didn't want to put you in the middle of things."

"As if I can't take care of myself."

"Brenda, I realize I still love Michael, but he's dishonest at times. I feel I can't trust him."

"I know about the amnesia thing, Maddy. But what you don't know is, Michael really did have amnesia at first. Once he realized the situation, he was afraid to tell you otherwise. From what Danny's said to me, he and Michael were working on so many plans, it's almost scary. Instead of feeling indignant, you should feel absolutely giddy that the man would go to so much trouble to win your affection."

"He told me he just wanted to be friends."

"That's bunk and you know it. The man loves you.

You love him. Now, when are you going to tell him about the baby?" When Maddy glanced away, she became insistent. "You *are* going to tell him, aren't you?"


Maddy's morning sickness worsened over the ensuing days, and although her obstetrician had offered to give her something during her first visit, she'd opted to wait. She didn't want to take any medication if she could help it, even if it had been proven safe.

"There's absolutely no reason to suspect a problem with this pregnancy," Dr. Flanders had told her, once she'd confessed her worries. "You're young and in perfect health. The morning sickness will pass, and the rest of the pregnancy should be a breeze."

Maddy had left the office feeling cheered.

The morning of the breakfast at Smyth-McGraw she was in her usual position, leaning over the toilet bowl, a wet washcloth in one hand. The soda crackers had done very little to settle her queasy stomach; she suspected part of it was nerves. She thought of canceling, but she knew she had to be there for Michael on his proud day. She owed him that much after all they'd meant to each other.

Michael had tried to contact her numerous times since their return from the cabin, but Maddy had avoided him. She had no idea what to do about the baby, and until she made a decision, she wanted as little contact with Michael as possible. Besides, this business of being friends was ridiculous. After five years living under the same roof, she could not think of Michael in those terms. She would not be able to look at him without remembering what it was like to lie in his arms after making love or smell his aftershave on his pillow once he'd left for work.

Maddy dressed in a chestnut-colored, sand-washed silk suit with matching pumps. Instead of pinning her hair up in a more professional look, she let it fall to her shoulders in natural waves and curls. As she started out the door she tucked her crackers in her purse and prayed she wouldn't need them.

When Maddy stepped into the lobby of Smyth-McGraw, she was surprised to find Michael waiting for her. The look on his face took her breath away. "Oh, honey, I'm so glad you're here. Thank you for coming." His hand was warm and strong as he grasped hers. "You look absolutely stunning."

His compliment was music to her ears after the way she'd been feeling. "Thank you, Michael. And congratulations on your promotion. I know you must be thrilled. And I'm thrilled for you. I'm sure your whole family is thrilled." She was chattering like an idiot, and he was looking at her as though he delighted in every word.

"We've got a few minutes," he said. "Would you like to see my new office?"

"I'd love to."

"Maddy?"

"Yes, Michael?"

"There's no need to be nervous." He smiled and squeezed her hand reassuringly as he guided her to the elevators and punched the button. "I've tried to reach you at work several times," he said. "Did you get my messages?"

"Yes, but I've been swamped with work, you see. One of the instructors relocated to another branch, so I've had to pick up the slack."

"I wanted to let you know you've had an offer on the condo, and it's pretty close to the asking price. The realtor hasn't been able to reach you either. I know you asked me to handle it, but I don't feel comfortable accepting an offer when it's not even my place."

"It's as much yours as it is mine," she said. "It was a wedding gift, remember?"

He started to respond, but a bell dinged, and one of the elevators whisked open. They stepped inside. Maddy could not get over her handsome husband in a smartly tailored suit. No matter how professional he looked—and he indeed epitomized what a senior partner should look like—there was still an inherent strength and masculinity about him that made her yearn to touch his cheek or run her fingers through his thick hair.

The elevator jolted upward with a whoosh, and Maddy's stomach went with it. She gripped the handrail.

"Sorry," Michael said, reaching out to steady her. "It's an old building, but you'd never convince these guys to move into something new and modern. Are you okay, Maddy?" His dark eyebrows drew together in a concerned expression.

"Oh, yes, I'm fine. I just wasn't expecting it."

"You look pale, honey. And you've lost weight."

He would lose weight, too, if he threw up everything he ate, she wanted to tell him, but didn't. She wished he'd stop being so nice to her. She was so emotional these days, she cried over just about everything. "I've been a little under the weather, that's all. I'm better now."

"And you've been doing somebody's job on top of being sick? I don't like it, Maddy. Not one bit."

He looked so serious, she almost smiled. "I'm not a fragile little teacup, Michael."

"I've just worried about you since, you know, what we went through in the mountains. That was pretty tough on all of us."

"Trust me. I'm strong as an ox."

The elevator stopped abruptly. This time Maddy's stomach went in the opposite direction, and her head seemed to spin like a top out of control. She stood motionless for one moment as everything whirled and blurred. She thought she heard Michael call her name before she blacked out.

Michael saw her going down and reached for her, catching her safely before she hit the ground. The elevator door swished open, and he swept her up high in his arms and hurried toward his new office. His secretary blinked in surprise as he strode past. "Call nine-one-one, Mrs. Kearns."

When Maddy family came to, she found herself stretched out on a luxurious sofa, a blanket covering her legs. Michael was beside her, giving orders to his secretary by way of his speakerphone. "Mrs. Kearns, please call Mr. Smyth and tell him I can't make the breakfast. My wife needs me."

He turned toward Maddy. "Oh, honey, you're awake. You scared me to death, and when you didn't come to right away, I suspected the worst."

"Michael, I need to talk to you," she said, unable to keep secrets from him any longer. "I've something to tell—"

A sharp rap at the door interrupted her. Two men walked in with a stretcher and various other medical equipment. They took one look at Maddy sprawled on the sofa and hurried over.

"What's the problem, ma'am?" a serious-looking man in uniform asked.

"I don't know why my husband's making such a fuss," Maddy said. "I just fainted."

The paramedic began taking her blood pressure while his partner shined a light in each of her eyes. "Did she strike her head when she fell?"

"No, I caught her," Michael told them. "But she was very pale. She says she just got over the flu."

"There's a lot of that going around." The man pulled out a tongue depressor.

Maddy shot a pleading look in Michael's direction as her throat was examined. The other paramedic pulled out a stethoscope and listened to her heart.

"Ma'am, are you on any prescription medicine or taking any other kind of drug?"

Michael instantly took offense. "My wife is not a drug addict, if that's what you're implying."

"Just doing our job, sir. We have to ask."

"I'm on prenatal vitamins," Maddy said.

"That doesn't sound illegal to me," Michael snapped, glaring at the paramedic. Suddenly he swung his head in Maddy's direction. "What? You're taking what?"

"How far are you into the pregnancy, ma'am?" the man asked.

"Not even six weeks yet. I've had terrible morning sickness, so I can't hold anything in my stomach in the morning or early afternoon. I've lost a few pounds, but my doctor assures me it'll pass. I guess it just got the better of me today."

"You're pregnant?" Michael sputtered, losing some of his polish as he tried to come to grips with the news.

"Yes, Michael."

Stunned, he slumped into a nearby chair. "She's going to have a baby," he told the paramedics. "I'm going to be a father." They seemed amused. Michael looked at her. "Are you sure?" he asked.

"Positive."

All at once he jumped to his feet. "We need to get her to a hospital," he told the paramedics.

"I don't need to go to the hospital, Michael," she said. "I just need to eat something."

"You can have anything you want, babe," he said, snatching up the phone.

"Applesauce would be nice," she said, "or some fresh fruit."

Michael relayed the message to his secretary. "Oh, and Mrs. Kearns, please order me a box of cigars. I'm going to be a father."

"I don't see any need to rush you to the ER unless you think you need to go," one of the paramedics told Maddy. "But I'd advise you to contact your doctor right away. He may want to give you something for your nausea. You're supposed to be gaining weight, not losing it."

"I'll give him a call," Maddy promised.

They finished their paperwork, congratulated the expectant couple, and were on their way in a matter of minutes. She glanced over at Michael and found him staring at her.

"Are you okay?" Maddy asked softly.

"You weren't even going to tell me, were you? You were going to go ahead with the divorce without telling me there was a baby."

"No, I—"

He gave a bitter laugh. "Well, I can't say that I blame you after the way I reacted last time." He crossed the room to stare out the window. "I can't do anything more to show you how much I love you, Maddy. That's why I handed in my resignation. I figured if I went out on my own, I could choose my own hours. That way I'd have more time for you and a family when we decided to start one."

Maddy couldn't mask her surprise. "You resigned?"

"That's right. That's when Smyth made me a senior partner." He continued to stare out the window. The day looked bleak. "But that's not good enough, is it? It doesn't make up for the past."

Maddy realized she had tears in her eyes. The old Michael would never have turned in his resignation. Not for her, not for anybody.

He sighed. "I can't change what happened in the past, Maddy, and I'm not going to spend my future begging your forgiveness. I've forgiven myself, and I suppose it'll have to be enough."

He turned and started for the door, and it was obvious he was having a hard time keeping his emotions under control. "I'll check on that applesauce."

"Michael, wait. . . ." Maddy raised up from the couch and walked toward him.

Her eyes were liquid as she looked into his. "I've already forgiven you," she said softly. "But can you ever find it in your heart to forgive me?"

He hesitated briefly before hauling her up into his arms and kissing her deeply. Maddy's kisses were just as hungry as she tried to convey all the love and devotion she felt for this wonderful husband of hers.

Michael broke the kiss briefly and stared into her face. Tears misted his eyes. "I want us to start over, Maddy. Our relationship, and our marriage."

"Are you saying we should go on with the divorce?"

"Hell no, I'm putting a stop to that today. After I take you to the doctor. There will be no divorce in this family."

She smiled. "So what are you suggesting?"

"I want us to go away somewhere, just the two of us, and renew our vows. It'll be even better than the first time because we won't have all that pomp and fuss that your parents put us through." His look turned tender. "Will you marry me, Maddy? All over again?"

"I'd consider it an honor," she replied.


A week later Michael and Maddy Kelly exchanged their vows in a small chapel in the North Carolina mountains, in the presence of an elderly minister, his wife, a mischievous-looking grandson, and two dachshunds whose tails thumped against the back of the front pew during the ceremony.

Maddy wore a champagne-colored suit and matching hat, and her husband was dressed in a navy suit with a white carnation at his lapel. Neither could keep their eyes off the other. And once they were pronounced husband and wife for the second time, they raced from the church, hand in hand, with the dogs following behind, to begin a two-week-long honeymoon. They laughed when they spied Michael's car. Old shoes and tin cans were tied to the back. Written across the rear windshield were the words JUST MARRIED AGAIN. One glance at the grandson, and they instantly knew who was responsible for it.

"Does this mean I should refer to you as my second husband?" Maddy asked.

"As long as I'm the last," Michael said, and smacked her on the bottom while the preacher and his wife looked on from the doorway of the church.

And when they reached their cabin, Michael carried his wife over the threshold, pausing inside only long enough to build a fire and give the "kids" a new steak-flavored bone while his wife put fresh sheets on the sofa bed and poured them each a toast from a grape-juice bottle. Michael undressed her in front of a roaring fire and took delight in the shadows that played across her naked body. He knelt before her and kissed her tummy, saying a silent prayer for the tiny being inside.

The moment brought tears to Maddy's eyes, just as so many other things did these days: aftershave commercials, split ends, a wet newspaper on the doorstep.

Lying beside her, Michael gazed at his wife lovingly.

Maddy's pregnancy had brought out all of his protective instincts. Although the doctor insisted exercise was good for her, Michael absolutely refused to let her teach the advanced aerobics classes. He'd made fast friends with the new fitness instructor and asked him to make sure Maddy didn't take any risks. So far she was behaving, probably because Michael had threatened to throw her over his shoulder and carry her out if he caught her doing anything she shouldn't. He knew she was being cautious. She wanted this baby as much as he did.

Now, as he kissed her breasts, he took great care since they were especially tender these days. He didn't know if it was his imagination, but they already felt heavier to him. He'd spent eighty bucks on an oversize book that covered every detail of pregnancy, and he already had a good idea what their baby looked like.

He'd even found time to read up on mood swings, just so he'd have a better understanding of what his wife was going through. He'd found it helpful when she'd burst into tears as they'd watched a sunset two days ago from the front porch of her little country house. Afterward, Michael had held her in his arms and promised to take her out for a banana split, and that seemed to make everything okay. He hoped her moods stopped swinging before they both grew as big as a barn.

He squeezed her nipples lightly, and she shivered. He captured her hand and moved it to his sex. She stroked him while he slipped his own hand between her thighs and parted her. He kissed her. Their legs became entwined, his long and hair-roughened, hers silky smooth.

Their coupling was a thing of beauty. When Michael finally entered her, Maddy arched high to meet him. As he began to drive deeply she cupped his buttocks and held him to her, half-afraid he might pull away and end the extreme pleasure he gave. She needn't have worried; he had no intention of going anywhere. They climaxed together and drifted back down to earth in each other's arms.

Some minutes later Michael raised up on one elbow and gazed down lovingly at his wife. "We're going to have the most beautiful baby in the world," Michael said. 'But then, how could it not be beautiful when the mother is as gorgeous as you?"

Maddy smiled and snuggled closer against his chest, enjoying the way the springy curls tickled her nose. God, how she loved the man. How had she ever managed to get through the long days and nights of their separation without talking to him or gazing into those dark eyes? She was determined to see this marriage succeed no mater what.

They lay there for a long time, talking, cuddling, sharing kisses. Michael told her what it had been like for him with her gone, and as Maddy listened she struggled to hold back her tears. She hadn't realized how barren she'd felt inside until Michael cloaked her in his love once more.

As she drifted off to sleep Maddy remembered a time, many years before, when nannies and housekeepers had spent hours primping her so that she would be acceptable to her mother and father once they sent for her. Somehow, she never felt she measured up. And then there was the time she'd asked Yates if he would teach her a funny joke so she could amuse her weary parents when they returned from a long trip. She hadn't been able to make them laugh.

Thankfully, it no longer mattered.

In her heart, she knew the man beside her would always love her unconditionally.

# FIFTEEN

Michael pulled into the driveway of his and Maddy's renovated farmhouse and was instantly greeted by a six-month-old, chocolate Lab pup, whom he'd adopted from the animal shelter because he felt a man should have a real dog. Maddy could have her spoiled, afraid-of-their-own-shadow dachshunds, he had Jack.

"Hey, boy," he said, stopping to pet his buddy on the head. By the size of his feet, he figured ol' Jack would grow to be the size of a Shetland pony. And he didn't lie around all day like those lazy hounds of Maddy's. Jack was fast becoming a good watchdog, and Michael liked knowing his girls were being looked after while he was away. Even as protective as he was of his wife, Michael was fiercely so where his baby daughter was concerned.

As Michael started up the front walk he spied their goat, Houdini, chewing on the azalea bushes. He shook his head sadly. As much as he loved his and Maddy's antebellum-style home, the goat was a constant annoyance. But the previous owners had insisted the creature was part of the bargain, and Maddy had fallen in love with him, so there was no getting out of it. They'd also inherited a couple of horses, a dozen or so chickens, and an aging bull named Geronimo, who was spending his retirement years grazing in the far pasture and napping under a tall oak tree.

Michael wouldn't have minded the goat so much had he been able to build a pen or fence to hold him, but none existed. Which is how Henry came to be called Houdini. He could break out of anything.

"Go ahead and eat my azalea bushes, pal," Michael said. "Because that's going to be your last meal. I'm going to get my bow and arrow out and—"

The front door opened and Maddy stepped out onto the porch. "Honey, who are you talking to?"

Michael had trouble swallowing these days when he saw his wife. Dressed as she was in a rose-colored, terrycloth jumpsuit, with her hair falling softly past her shoulders, one would never have guessed she'd given birth to a nine-pound daughter just six weeks prior. Except for her breasts, of course, which were pleasantly plump with breast milk. He actually became aroused thinking about them.

"Michael?"

"Huh? Oh, I was just having a little talk with Houdini. Telling him about my day."

Maddy folded her arms in front of her. "You haven't been threatening him again? You know how crazy I am about that goat."

"And so am I, babe. Actually, I was just explaining

there was a whole shipment of azalea bushes coming in on Saturday."

She tried to look stern, but it wasn't easy with her husband standing there looking sexier than any man had a right. "You know the rules of the house."

"Be nice to your goat and no briefcases allowed in the house. The guys at the office say I'm henpecked. Well, they call it something else, but it means the same thing."

She offered him her hand. "I say they're jealous."

He grinned and backed her against the door frame. "Yeah, big time." He placed his hands on her shoulders and kissed her deeply, pressing against her so she could feel his need. When he raised up, there was a question in his eyes. "Did you go to the doctor today?" he asked, knowing she'd had an appointment for her six-week checkup.

"Yes."

"And?"

"He says I've healed nicely."

Michael's stomach seemed to take a giant swoop. His mouth went bone-dry. "Oh, yeah?"

Maddy grabbed his tie and pulled him into the house, closing the door and locking it securely behind him. The large living room had been painted a soft mint green and trimmed in antique white. The furniture was covered in a mint, yellow, and white plaid with sprigs of ivy. She led Michael to the sofa and pushed him down.

"Now, you sit right there and relax while I finish the hors d'oeuvres. Dinner is going to be late tonight."

He reached for her hand. "I'm not hungry."

She pulled free. "Trust me. You're going to need your strength."

Michael swallowed as he watched her walk from the room. It was all he could do to keep himself from throwing her down on the floor and taking her there. He shook his head. The guys were right. She had him wrapped around her little finger and then some.

And he was loving every minute of it.

Unable to sit still, Michael made his way down the hall to the nursery. Very quietly, he entered the sweet-smelling room and crept softly toward the antique white crib. His six-week-old daughter was sleeping on her back, her tiny fists balled at her side. Her cheeks were chubby and rosy, her light downy hair curling about her face.

Maddy had insisted on naming her Kathleen, after his mother, but they called her Katy. Michael had never seen such perfection before, and his heart swelled with love and pride as he gazed down at her. Danny claimed she took after him, although Michael saw traces of Maddy in her too. He could not believe there was a time when he hadn't wanted children. Heck, he was already looking forward to giving little Katy a brother.

As much as he wanted to pick her up, he knew this was not the time. Later he would feed her a bottle of breast milk that Maddy pumped each day for just that reason. And when it came time for her bath, he would assist Maddy, and they would laugh at their daughter's antics because she had not yet learned to like water.

Right now he had more pressing business.

He was going to make mad passionate love to little Katy's mother.

# THE EDITORS' CORNER

How often do you read a really good book? We hope that with LOVESWEPT, you read four. Per month. This month we're taking you on a trip around the country with four delightful romances from some of our best authors. From love on the range to the streets of New York and Dallas and the heart of the South, you're off on a journey of the heart.

The first gem is Marcia Evanick's **SILVER IN THE MOONLIGHT**, LOVESWEPT #906. Dean Warren Katz had nothing but the best of intentions when he wrote to Katherine Silver regarding the welfare of her aunts. He was just being neighborly to the little old ladies whose house was ready to cave in. When Katherine arrived in Jasper, South Carolina, it didn't take a genius to see that her aunts were hale and hearty. Now if she could just get her hands around Mr. Katz's neck. But he tells her to look below the surface, at the furniture placed to hide cracks in the walls, the broken shutters, not to mention the crumbling foundation, well hidden by a generous array of bushes. Sharing coffee, conversation, and a whole lot more, Dean and Katherine launch a crusade to renovate the house. Marcia Evanick's latest book is rich with romance, and highly reminiscent of mint juleps, old porches, rocking chairs, and, of course, starry southern nights.

RaeAnne Thayne returns with **SWEET JUSTICE**, LOVESWEPT #907. Somehow Nicholas Kincaid can't believe Ivy Parker when she says that he wouldn't even notice the 500 sheep she wants to raise on his land. Ivy's ranch is already dangerously close to bankruptcy, and without the fresh grass on Kincaid's land, she'll have to sell off part of the herd to buy food for the rest. Nick is her only hope, but all he wants is some peace and quiet. Lord knows he needs it—he's spent the past year trying the most-watched case since the O. J. Simpson trial. Nick's motto is Don't get involved, but when he learns how desperate Ivy's situation is, he relents. Now her problems are his as well, and suddenly, being neighbors isn't so bad. And as he watches Ivy stand her ground against the rumors and mysterious occurrences on the ranch, he realizes that in her he may have found the home he's never known. RaeAnne Thayne weaves a sensual and moving tale of passion and intrigue on the range.

Fayrene Preston tells us Kylie Damaron's story in **THE DAMARON MARK: THE LOVERS**, LOVESWEPT #908. Contrary to popular belief, you can go home again, and David Galado has done just that—much to Kylie's dismay. From the time she was a little girl, Kylie had depended on David to be her fierce protector from the dark shadows that had haunted her life. A chance encounter and misunderstandings had reduced them to mere acquaintances, a pretense that David had always tried to uphold. But when David learns of Kylie's new boyfriend, a man with dangerous connections, he can't stop himself from getting involved. Kylie's wondered a thousand times over about what would have happened if David had never left in the first place, and here's her chance to find out. But when an attempt on her life is made, will she allow herself to trust her heart and her future to a man she once thought she loved? Fayrene Preston answers that question when two lost souls throw fate to the wind and find solace in each other.

In **HOT PROPERTY**, LOVESWEPT #909, Karen Leabo pits a tough-talking detective against his awfully beautiful suspect. For Wendy Thayer, turning thirty is rough, but getting arrested on her birthday has got to take the cake. Despite all her objections to the contrary, Michael Taggart hauls Wendy into the station house on charges of transporting stolen goods. But the beautiful personal shopper insists that she and her favorite client are innocent of any wrongdoing. And once she's located Mr. Neff, she'll prove it, she promises. Wendy knows there's been a huge mistake, sweet Mr. Neff just couldn't be a criminal. But as Michael and Wendy search for the elusive old man, more clues keep popping up to incriminate Wendy. Michael has learned to distrust any woman who loves to spend money, never mind a woman who does it for a living. But when the odds are against them, will he gamble away his dreams for the chance to be with Wendy? In a delightful tale of passionate pursuit, Karen Leabo sends two unlikely lovers on a journey to discover their own unspoken longings.

Happy reading!

With warmest wishes,

*Susann Brailey*    *Joy Abella*

Susann Brailey          Joy Abella
Senior Editor           Administrative Editor